Copyright (

All ri,

The characters and events portrayed in this book are
fictitious. Any similarity to real persons, living or dead, is
coincidental and not intended by the author.

No part of this book may be reproduced, or stored in a
retrieval system, or transmitted in any form or by any
means, electronic, mechanical, photocopying, recording,
or otherwise, without express written permission of the
publisher.

ISBN: 9798390949597

Cover design by: Alisha Ritchie

CONTENTS

ACKNOWLEDGEMENT

To my mum, for believing in me when no one else did.

To my sister, for supporting me through all the ups and downs.

To Alisha for an amazing cover.

To the many tutors, who encouraged me to follow my dreams.

Thank you for everything.

MOLLIE SYKES

CHAPTER 1

My hands grip the wheel as I drive down the deserted country roads. Watching the trees and scenery pass by, should be nostalgic and calming, but it isn't. My eyes stay glued to the empty roads as I try to tell myself that this is a good idea. Part of me can't wait to finally arrive, but another part of me is screaming that this isn't going to end well. I mean leaving a well-paid job in accounting and a lovely home to move to the middle of nowhere, sounds like a crazy idea. But after Jack left me for some other woman, I was itching for a change.

I'd been looking at houses to buy since the money from my divorce was rather hefty. Obviously, I didn't want to be anywhere near Jack, so I'd been scrolling through housing agencies, when I came across my childhood home for sale.

It just seemed like it was meant to be.

After my mother and father died in an accident when I was 20, I'd never been back there. The house was sold to a couple, and I never gave it much thought after that. But when it came up for sale right at the time I needed a change, I started thinking.

Alright, it's a big change to move to a town with not a lot going on. But it's a community. It's the community environment, I missed dearly. Living in a city it was an each to their own mentality. But not my hometown. Here everyone knows everyone, which does have its drawbacks but ultimately, it's amazing having people around you who will support and protect you. The crime rate is very low, since neighbours protect neighbours. I'm sure there's still some unsavoury people around, but that's going to happen anywhere.

"Freyja, don't get me wrong," my long-time friend Jillian calls out through the speaker phone, "I'm excited you're coming back to town, but are you sure you want to?" For the millionth time she asks me and for the millionth time I try to assure myself that this is exactly what I should do.

I try to reason with her as much as myself saying, "I've never had a problem with the town, and I know it's a lot slower than what I'm used to, but it is the right thing."

"But what about … you know… the incident?" she asks, knowing the reason I had left town in the first place.

My hands grip the steering wheel tightly. Breathing deep, I exhale slowly whilst loosening my vice-like grip.

"It's been 7 years," I explain. "I've had time to deal with it."

Despite it still being a tough subject, I really have gotten over it. It just took time. Now I'm older and wiser and trained in multiple forms of martial arts, it isn't likely to be repeated.

I keep my eyes focused on the empty road. Since this isn't the first time I've driven around here, I know for a fact that, just because it's empty, it doesn't mean animals don't skitter across. I wouldn't be able to live with myself if I hurt one, even if it was an accident.

"Okay. If you're sure," Jill sighs into the phone, "I can't wait to see you again, it's been way too long."

A small chuckle comes out of me. "Really? Is two weeks classed as too long now?" I remark.

Despite us living hours away from each other, we still make time to visit. Usually, we meet in the middle and stay at a hotel, rather than one of us having to travel the full distance.

"Yes," she screeches. "A day is too long not to see my sister from another mister... and miss," she adds chuckling.

We are by no means related, but growing up together we formed an unbreakable bond and we behaved and treated each other like sisters. In fact, even both of our parents used to treat us like sisters, and neither would so much as blink if we showed up at either house. In fact, there were times I even went to Jill's house whilst she was away on holiday. I said hi to her parents and we had tea together. Then I went home, although they had said I could stay the night if I wanted. So, we are sisters. Even if not by blood.

"Anyway, got any juicy gossip to fill me in on?" I ask remembering how jittery Jill was, the last time we spoke. "How about that hottie who you spoke about last time?"

"He's in town. Staying at the creepy estate," she adds.

I'd forgotten about that damn mansion. It should have stuck out like a sore thumb, considering it's pretty much the size of a castle and not even a small one at that, and yet it seemed to fit in perfectly with the town. Everyone knew it was owned by some weird recluse. A couple of times Jill and I dared one another to sneak onto the property, but we were always found, and after the threat of a smack with the belt neither of us did it again.

"He must know the owner," I say, my eyes still plastered to the empty road. "I've never known anyone to visit that place. Then again for all we know it's actually empty. I've never seen any signs of life." My fingers tap along mindlessly to the quiet music coming from the radio.

She whines, "Who the hell knows? But I did see him. Why is it the hot ones are always way out of my league?"

Shaking my head and rolling my eyes at her antics, I take a turn. I make it part way down the road when I swerve to avoid the car racing down. The road's barely big enough for one car, so it doesn't take much for me to drive into some bushes.

Blaring my horn at the arsehole driver, I screech out, "What the hell, arsehole? Fucking piece of fucking shit trying to fucking kill us!"

"Are you alright?" Jill asks.

Panting and clutching the wheel tight again I say, "Just some idiot speeding." Taking a deep breath, I slowly get back on the road and carry on driving.

Just as the pounding in my chest slows, I

spot a car driving behind me. It's a familiar red car. It's the prick who just nearly crashed into me. With my blood heating in my veins, I say, "Give me a minute Jill."

Slowly I pull the car to a stop in the centre of the road, forcing the car following to stop.

Opening my door, I climb out with what I'm sure is the fiery pits of hell shining in my eyes. The woman in the sporty red car clambers out in her heels and far too short dress. The expression on her face doesn't bode well for this going smoothly.

"Bitch, you nearly hit my car," the blonde woman screeches.

She did not just say that.

"Well maybe if you weren't speeding, YOU wouldn't have nearly hit ME," I shout, the blood in my veins pumping. "I was going the speed limit."

"You were in my way," she screeches.

Does this bitch seriously not have anything other than that lame-ass line to say?

Deciding the bitch needs to learn a lesson for her idiocy, I waltz up to her car, whilst pulling out my multi-tool from my bag. Sticking the knife into the tyre, I smile sweetly saying, "I suggest you learn how to drive. There's plenty of wildlife out here that you could hurt as well as other people driving. The world doesn't revolve around you," I explain.

Apparently, that wasn't what the bitch wanted to hear. As I'm walking back to my car, a hand clutches onto my long black hair and the bitch screeches in anger. Batting out with reflexes, I push my elbow into her gut. She lets go of my hair, curling over, gasping. Again, I move towards my car, only she trips me, and I fall to the ground. Jumping up, my fist swings out and clocks her in the face. She screeches and, as she goes to swing at me, I duck sending a foot flying towards her ribs.

This time she doesn't stand back up. She lays there too stunned to move.

Climbing back into the car I carry on with my journey, jumping slightly when I hear Jill through the speaker. I forgot she was still on the phone.

"Sorry about that Jill. The idiot who nearly killed me had circled back to shout at me for almost hitting her car. As though I was the one speeding like a jackass," I explain.

"Ouch. Sounds like it was painful for her. You didn't actually start a fight... did you?" she asks, sounding concerned.

"I didn't start it. I merely finished it," I answer innocently. "Although I may have slashed a tyre."

"Right. Let me guess, it was because she showed no consideration or care for the wildlife?" she asks, and an amused grin lights up my face. She knows me well enough to know I will speak my mind when the safety of animals is concerned. Safety of people is important, but animals are innocent. People very rarely are. The only exception is kids.

"Of course. Anyway, I'll speak later. I'm nearly at the house," I say. With quick goodbyes we hang up.

As I pull into the property, memories come flooding back. The time I learnt to ride a bike and had run into the large tree, that still stands to this day, because I wasn't watching where I was going. Or the time I helped my dad build the tree house, that is now in a slight state of disrepair from not being maintained. A small smile stretches my face.

Even after seven years the property hasn't changed all that much. Two floors, a wraparound porch, a brown rocking chair swaying gently with the breeze. It was obviously left by the previous occupants, but it's exactly like it was when I was a child.

I enter the house and smile as even more memories come flooding in. The games night my mother, father and I used to have. The way they would always let me win, not wanting me to be sad about losing. How my grandmother and me would sit at a low table doing a jigsaw puzzle together. She'd always let me put the last piece in.

Now it's an empty shell. New carpets have already been put in, and the walls have already been painted. I'll have to remember to thank Jill for sorting it all for me. I've gone with neutral colours as the colour will come with the décor.

I head upstairs and straight to the master room. The room that once belonged to my mum and dad. On a weekend, I used to wake up and come into their room to see if they were awake. If they were still asleep, I used to get into bed with them and doze off. As I got older, I would attempt to make them breakfast in bed. As an adult, I know Bailey's isn't a morning drink, at least not if you're driving. As a child, I thought that was a perfectly acceptable drink. That's the day they explained what alcohol is. The love they had for me was never-ending and I miss them every day.

This room is now mine. It feels wrong in a way, but at the same time it's the only room with an ensuite and it's also the only bedroom with a walk-in wardrobe. Of course I'm going to use it. One day I hope to have kids, and the idea of raising my children in the house I was raised in, brings a soft smile to my face.

A knock sounds on the door. Once downstairs, I open the door to find Jillian stood there with a bottle of wine, cakes and a huge grin. She also has an unknown man with her. She squeals as her arms go around my neck, being careful not to break the bottle or crush the food. I wrap my arms around her and squeeze all the air from her. Just this one connection and I feel like I'm home.

"I thought I'd come by early and help you unpack," she offers. "Obviously it can't be accomplished without sustenance," she adds holding up the booze and cake. She's the best.

When I look to the man next to her, she chuckles again.

"Sorry. Freyja, meet Dixon. Dixon this is my sister Freyja," she introduces. "He helped me unload your things from storage and has offered to help bring everything in. He also has the rest of the booze." Sure enough, he has a bag in his hand that clinks as he moves.

"Come on in. I would say I'll get the glasses, but I have no idea where they are," I remark.

"We bought plastic cups," Dixon grins, picking up some red plastic cups from inside the bag. That was excellent thinking on their part.

With our cups filled and pastries eaten, we get to work unpacking the car and trailer. It takes hours to unload everything, but by the end we have all the boxes and furniture in the right rooms, ready to start unpacking. We're also out of pastries.

"I'll order take out whilst you two go and sort the bed out," Dixon offers.

It's the one thing that needs to be sorted today. Since it's getting pretty late, we'll need to be finishing up soon. Jill and I head upstairs to the master room, where my bed is ready to be assembled, with the mattress against the wall. Screw it, I decide. A mattress on the floor will be good enough for tonight.

Before Jill can even ask, I pull the mattress to the ground and open the bag with my new duvet in. Jill gets the bag with my bedding opened without me needing to ask and within 20 minutes we have my bed sorted for the night.

When the food arrives, we all sit on the ground and dig in. I still need to buy a new sofa, since my other one was given to Jack. It would have been too much to bring that with me. I'd have had to hire movers instead of just piling everything into cars. Jill has truly been my lifesaver for this move, since she drove up to my house so she could take some of my belongings with her and put it into storage. I don't know how I could ever repay her.

"What's your plan now?" Dixon asks politely.

I look up to him with a mouthful of food.

"She already has a job lined up," Jill answers for me. "She's working at Sue's Sanguine Sweets."

His eyes go wide, and he gives a nod of well done. The shop is new, or at least new enough that I can't remember it from when I was last here. Judging by what Jill said after I got the job, the owner can be very protective and doesn't often hire any help. The only reason she hired me in particular was because of the overwhelming assurance of the community that I would be a good fit.

"So, tell us about this bitch who nearly killed you," Jill adds, and Dixon seems to get infuriated by this news. Despite him not knowing me, I get the feeling he's protective of everyone and is a true gentleman.

"She was speeding, and I swerved to avoid her. That's all," I remark. "Oh, and obviously she circled round to rip into me for 'nearly hitting her'. I taught her the errors of her ways."

"Anyway, I think we should call it a night. I'm knackered," I say.

It was decided that they would sleep here, since they both offered to help me tomorrow to unpack.

CHAPTER 2

Yawning, I make my way into the bakery. 7am seems far too early to be at work, but whatever. Sue did tell me that it wouldn't be this early again, it's just to get me situated and explain everything. I know from experience our small town runs later than most. The shops don't often open until 1pm and close around 9pm. It's never seemed odd to me, since I grew up here, although it was certainly a shock when I moved towns and had to be at work at 8am. I never did like that schedule.

"Good morning, Sunshine," says Sue an older lady, likely in her late 60's.

"Morning," I offer, as another yawn escapes.

I chug down some more of the coffee in my travel flask.

"So, we'll get right to it. The counter shows the two ranges of products we offer. Everything from this side, you'll be responsible for making. Everything on this side, I make. Deal?" she asks, and I nod my head.

The pastries seem similar on either side, although the ones on her side have an odd colour. Maybe it's a different flavour, or maybe even free from different allergens.

"I typically prepare what I can when we close up," She explains. "Then in the morning I only have to bake them. The recipes are all on the counter in the back although once you've baked them enough times, you'll likely not need them," she chuckles.

We head in the back and get to work. She has already prepared a lot of the baked goods for today, so we get to work folding and shaping everything to go into the ovens. Once everything's cooked and set out, I get to work preparing some more dough and batter for the many baked goods. It takes me longer than it takes Sue, but I suspect I'll get quicker as I gain more experience. It's odd baking something in such a large batch. Certainly not something I'm used to.

As we open the shop up, I'm surprised to see we get many customers come in, almost as soon as the door is open. Sue helps to explain the sales as we go. Teaching me how to use the cash machine, and how to box everything properly.

"Hi, I'd like to place an order," A customer states. "200 dead gingerbread, 200 red whipped cupcakes and also 250 of the custard slices," she explains, and I jot down the information.

"Is it delivery or pick up and what date?" I ask the ethereal looking woman.

"Pick up, and it will be for Saturday," she explains, and I nod my head.

Sue had explained she does orders, and that orders containing more than 5 types of baked goods, or with a total quantity of over 1000 should be run by her, but other than that we're good to go. I honestly have no idea how this woman could cope without help. Today it's been busy, and we've not stopped, and that's with two of us here. At the moment I'm serving as she bakes some more, since we're running low. How did she do this when she was by herself?

"Alright, it should be ready for 1pm," I explain going by what Sue had told me. All orders must be ready by 1pm by the day of delivery or pick up.

"Thank you," she says before heading out.

By the time we close up my feet ache,

my arms ache and I'm ready to sleep. But still, we must go on and prepare what we can for tomorrow. It takes another two hours after closing for us to have gotten as much as we can prepared for tomorrow. Now I understand why she closes at 8pm, otherwise it would be very late before we get home.

Apparently, the preparation went quicker than it usually does since there was two of us. Overall, she seems happy with me. We collect our things before locking up.

"I'll see you at 11am tomorrow," she smiles warmly.

With a quick goodbye, I head in the direction of the cemetery. I've put it off long enough and I promised myself I would visit once I had settled in.

The night is quiet, with only the trees rustling in the breeze disturbing the peace. It's pleasant. The moon sits high in the sky illuminating the path in front of me. The gate to the cemetery squeaks open and I make my way in.

I walk through the unfamiliar paths, until finally, I reach those I came to visit.

"Hey Mum, Dad, Gigi and Papi," I say into the quiet night, looking at the four headstones of those I love so dearly. "So, I've moved back. Jill and Dixon helped me unpack, and today I went to the bakery to start work. It was hard, but it was fun. The smell of pastries and cakes, however, had me drooling and wanting to eat them all, but I suppose that's nothing new," I explain.

I can almost imagine them laughing. It's as though I can hear Gigi say, "that sweet tooth will rot 'em if you're not careful." I obviously never listened to her. Then again, she was just as bad, and we certainly know who I inherited my love of sweet stuff from.

"I also nearly got hit by an idiot speeding. But don't worry, I harnessed the power of dad and Gigi and ripped into the bitch for being so stupid," I add, chuckling. I know that my parents would be thrilled to know I taught her a lesson. Although they would probably be less than thrilled to learn I decked her.

The laughter I know would have bubbled out of them all, rings in my ears. That sound will forever be engrained in me since we laughed hard and often. It's the sound I miss the most because it was the music that bought me the most comfort.

"I'm telling you, he's furious," I hear someone say. It sounds like a man. Turning around I spot the group and I don't know what possesses me to do so, but I hide behind a headstone hoping they won't notice me.

"Someone hit his woman and she still hasn't healed from it. Whoever she got in a fight with, should run for the hills."

"Shut up, Mal. Everyone knows he isn't going to last long enough to defend his whore, who we all know deserved a black eye or two," a woman says.

My brow scrunches.

"Don't let the councilman hear you say that he'd have your guts for garters," who I'm assuming is Mal, says. This sounds rather violent. I have to hold back a squeal as my bloodthirsty nature kicks in.

"Which part?" the woman says.

"That the King won't last long," Mal clarifies.

"Everyone knows that the kings who don't find their mate before their 100th birthday, die," another man chimes in.

"Please, that's a myth," a new woman offers in disbelief. She has long blonde hair and even from here I can see it falling in tresses down her back. I think I'll call her Blondie.

"It's a curse," the unnamed women explains seriously. I'm starting to think they've lost the plot.

"Holy shit. Are you wearing my skirt?" I hear blondie scream. As I look, I notice her eyes are pinned to the unnamed guy. "Hades, I swear to the devil himself if you're wearing my skirt, I will gut you," she screeches. Sure enough, the unnamed man, or I suppose Hades, is wearing an above knee skirt and seems to be rocking it.

"But it's so freeing. It lets the boys breathe," he explains without an ounce of concern. Just as they are about to start scrapping, I lean a little too far and fall on the ground with an 'oomph'.

I really hope they didn't hear me. If they did, they would know I was eavesdropping and that would be super awkward. Looking up, I find four sets of glowing eyes glued to me. All look furious. Wait... glowing. Surely that's got to be a trick of the eye. Blinking, the luminescence goes, and I inwardly sigh knowing I'm not going mad and letting the dark spooky atmosphere get to me.

"That skirt looks great on you," I remark, not thinking at all. Hades smiles brightly, looking at Blondie, in an 'I told you so' way.

"Were you listening in on us?" Mal asks looking... not annoyed. The way he furrows his brow makes him seem almost curious.

"Who? Me? No. No. Of course not. I just came to speak to the dead," I offer then wince.

"Not actually speak to them. Well technically I was speaking to them, but they didn't reply… probably for the best." I let out a nervous chuckle. What the hell has gotten into me? I sound like an awkward teenager.

"Right," Hades says with a small grin. "Well, if you have finished communing with the dead, I suggest you go home. It isn't safe after dark," he warns.

Despite not getting the sense he was being threatening, it still seems like a strong possibility. "Are you threatening me?" I ask coldly.

I'd be proud of how serious and stern I sounded, if not for the fact I'm practically vibrating with anger. Before he can reply, I dig around in my bag, whilst maintaining eye contact with the group. When my hands close around the metal canister, I breathe a sigh of relief. Slowly removing it from my bag, I hold it firmly in my hand.

"Not threatening you. Just warning you there are dangers around," he offers placatingly. Still the canister remains firmly in my grasp as I slowly attempt to back away from the group.

A low growl from behind me has me forgetting all about the group in front.

Spinning around, I hold out the canister. Even if it's an animal, pepper spray will still stun them.

"Get behind us," Hades says, worry tight in his voice.

My instincts have me moving towards them, never allowing my eyes to stray from the potential danger lurking in the shadows.

The fact my instincts have me moving to cower behind someone else, is concerning. But clearly my instincts know this isn't the sort of danger I'm equipped to deal with. That itself is concerning enough, since I am very highly trained in many forms of self-defence and martial arts.

A rustle has my eyes darting to the left, and before I even have time to scream, a hideous creature comes barrelling out towards me. The pepper spray is fired and the creature roars swiping out at me. Despite its grotesque and rotten image, it's surprisingly strong and has me flying through the air. I hit a tree with a sickening crunch and fall to the ground.

The four strangers get into gear and pull weapons from their persons that I didn't even know they carried. They work seamlessly together, dispatching the creature with practiced skill. Only when they are sure the creature won't get back up again, does their focus turn to me.

I flinch and attempt to move away from

them, only to realise I can't feel my legs.

A tear pricks my eye as these four warriors stalk my way with their weapons out. All I can do is lay there pleading with them not to kill me, but with no way of getting up and running off, I have no choice but to lay there. A wounded animal.

"Are you alright?" Mal asks, his eyes moving to the slashes across my chest from the creature. I'd completely forgot about them. He side eyes his friends in that telling way. I'm dying. Am I actually dying? I didn't imagine this was how I'd go.

Suddenly an intense pain rips through my chest. It would seem the adrenaline has started to fade. My back arches under the pressure and cracks and crunches rush through my body. A silent scream tears from my lips and my breath catches in my chest. I can feel the darkness creeping in.

Those around me are talking, but I can't figure out what it's about. As the darkness further encircles me, Hades lifts up my upper body and only the numbness prevents the pain. Something pierces my neck deeply, but again no sound escapes me. As a final tear slides warmly down my cold cheek, my eyes close and I sink into oblivion.

CHAPTER 3

Peeling my eyes open, I groan at the realisation it's already morning. Despite what must have been a deep sleep, I'm still tired. Rolling on my side, I look at the time on my phone, 11am. Thank God it's my day off or I would be late to work. Instead, my day will be taken up by unpacking. Oh, the joy.

Knowing if I don't move now, I will stay in bed all day, I roll out trying to get my uncooperative joints to move. As soon as I stand up, nausea ripples through me and I stumble my way to the bathroom, only just making it in time to throw up. I heave relentlessly, until my stomach is finally empty. Flushing the toilet, I put the lid down and rest my head against it. Where did that come from? I don't feel particularly ill, so it's probably just a bit of nausea from getting up too quickly.

I rinse my mouth out and after relieving my aching bladder and washing my hands, I head downstairs and flip on the kettle. It seems to take forever to boil, and I tap my foot impatiently as I wait. Once the tea is made, I barely wait for it to cool before chugging it down. When that doesn't wake me up, I prepare another one.

What the hell did I get up to last night to feel so rough? I'd gone to visit my parents and grandparents and …. My memories are a blank after that. That can't be a good thing.

Judging by the sickness and the tired feeling, my guess is alcohol. I've always been able to handle my drinks. It used to annoy my ex to no end when I would drink him under the table, and he'd make a fool out of himself. I don't mean he made a fool out of himself because I could drink more. It's more a case of he'd always try to one up me, even when we drank. He'd end up smashed and couldn't handle it.

Maybe I left the cemetery and got drunk. I'd have to have drunk a lot to have a memory blank, but it happened one other time. That's got to be it. I'll just ignore the fact that the memory blank I had a long time ago wasn't because of the booze…

After the incident in my past, I very really drank. I was always cautious and the only reason

I ever drank anything with my ex was because of peer pressure. I've no idea what could have possessed me to think drinking was a good option. It's not something I enjoy.

When a knock on the door rings out, I groan. Who the fuck's that? Most people don't head out until around noon. Sue and I only get up early to start baking. Our morning is the equivalent of getting to work for 5am. Or at least if we were to have the same hours as other towns.

Shuffling my way to the door, I unlock it and, maintaining my resting bitch face, open the door, only to find an upbeat smiling Jill. She holds up a box with Sue's Sanguine Sweets printed on the top. At least she didn't come empty handed.

"What?" I ask a grinning Jill.

"Morning, Sugar," She chirps with a grin lifting her cheeks.

"Urgh," I groan and head back into the kitchen where the life-giving substance lives.

"I see you're still as bright and chipper as ever in the morning," Jill jokes.

The glare I send her way, has her grinning like a loon. "Bitch," I mutter.

Once I've had another three cups of tea, a couple of cigarettes and some pastries, we crack on. I know, smoking's bad. It kills. Blah blah blah.

I should quit, but it isn't going to happen any time soon and I don't smoke often. Just when I'm in a particularly foul mood.

Eventually we start unpacking box after box, as well as putting up any bits of furniture we missed.

Lifting up a box that got put in the spare room instead of the garage, I'm surprised when it feels really light. I could have sworn Jill said it has my laundry detergents in. Surely it should be heavier than this. Shrugging it off, after all it's likely the bottles are emptier than I thought, I carry it downstairs. As I reach the bottom of the stairs, another knock sounds at the door, and I inwardly squeal at the chance to have a valid excuse to take a break.

Placing the box on the ground I make my way to the door. Opening the door, I smile politely at the two strangers.

"Hi, we're your neighbours from just down the way," the brunette middle-aged woman offers with a big grin. "We thought we'd come and introduce ourselves. I'm Maggie, and this is my husband, Jon," she introduces, indicating the blonde, pot-bellied man who tips his hat with a polite 'ma'am'.

I forgot how old school this town is. I seem to have forgotten a fair bit.

"Hi, I'm Freyja," I offer. Just as I say this, Jill comes barrelling down the stairs wanting to be nosy.

"Who is it?" she calls. Then once she sees the couple says, "Hey Maggie. Jon."

Of course, she knows who they are. Everyone knows everyone around here. That being said, I'm surprised how many new faces I'm seeing. I know I was never very social as a child, but even so, other than Jill's parents and a couple of locals, I don't really recognise anyone at the moment.

"Ma'am," Maggie and Jon both offer in greeting.

After letting them come in and offering them a drink, we sit down to chat. They both give off a friendly energy and nothing in me is concerned about their greeting. Still, I keep my eye on the pair. After all the security work I did in the city, I learnt to read body language well. Their body language tells me they're comfortable.

"So, Freyja where did you move from?" Maggie asks.

"I moved from the city," I explain.

Maggie gushes, "No way. You're a city girl? I'd never have expected that."

Jillian fills in by adding, "She was born and

raised here, so she isn't a city gal. Not really anyway. We hoped she'd come back." Jill looks at me with a soft unreadable expression. Whatever she's thinking isn't bad, but it's still something she's puzzling together.

Jon pulls me from my musings. "Why did you leave?" Jon asks. A crease forming in his brow.

I wince slightly and I notice Jillian do the same.

"I just felt like a change," I explain weakly. I mean it's not entirely a lie. After the incident, I decided to just go for it and leave the past in the past, but apparently, I couldn't stay away for long.

The memories of the incident have the mood in the room darkening. I'd tried my hardest to forget the entire thing. Obviously returning home did bring the risk of memories returning, but I didn't expect to still be so affected by them. I'd worked for years to get over it, but a little bit of time here and they feel as fresh as when it first happened.

"How did you cope in the city?" Maggie asks looking shocked and pulling me from my own mind. "I mean I know it's possible, but I could never..." she trails off looking to my right.

Looking in the direction Maggie is staring; I realise Jill is giving her the universal facial expression for shut the fuck up. What's that all about?

Jill's usually so outspoken and friendly. She's also the sort of person who can't keep a secret. Honestly, she's an amazing friend and I could trust her with anything, other than a secret. She starts talking and just doesn't stop, but it's never with malicious intent. If that was the case, I'd have beat the snot out of her and wouldn't have gotten upset about it. Still her expression is a sign she's keeping something from me.

Jill's always been weird and protective. Although it was always me who got into the fights, so I suppose there was a valid reason for her protective streak. Still, there's something niggling at the back of my mind that her reaction is stranger than usual. It's telling me there is something people are keeping from me, and if I don't find out soon, I suspect I'll blow up like I usually do.

Ignoring Jill's odd behaviour, I explain, "It was a big adjustment. They like to make the most out of the daylight hours and ignore the magic of the night, but I got used to it." It just took years for that to happen.

"That must have been difficult. What did you do for a living?" Jon offers conversationally, clearly wanting to move on from the odd exchange as well.

"I was in accounting for a couple of years. Before that, I worked in security," I explain.

Not adding the fact, that the only reason I quit the security work, was because Jack and I were going to start a family, and he didn't want me in a dangerous job that could harm his heir.

When we first met it was lovely, but as soon as we got married things changed. We spoke about having kids, but I didn't want to give up my security work. He then said I'd be an awful mother if I wasn't willing to give up a dangerous job to protect his heir. He even used the words 'his heir'. Things changed then, but I went along with it hoping it was just his mother hounding him. When it became obvious it wasn't just his mum butting into the situation, I left.

"What about you guys? What do you do for a living? When did you move here, I don't recognise you from when I was last here?"

"We were travelling for a while. About five years ago we came back knowing we would be needed soon," she says, and I frown. "I work in the library and Jon here works in the local police department," she explains proudly. But my mind is still stuck on the 'we would be needed soon'. Needed by who? Surely working as a librarian and a police officer doesn't require them to have to move here.

Maybe I've missed some part of the conversation while I was travelling down memory lane. It's not surprising since dredging up the past is bringing with it uncomfortable memories. It's not Maggie and Jon's fault. They're only being neighbourly.

Chuckling, Maggie says, "Anyway, we better get going. We didn't mean to take up so much of your time. Just thought we'd pop round to be neighbourly." The bubbly couple get up and leave the house.

Turning to Jill, I give her a raised brow. "She's so weird," I remark with a chuckle.

She smirks, "Yep. Most folks around here are. Or did you forget that as well?"

I nearly wince at the dig. Since moving here, I seem to be remembering everything that I'd suppressed or put to the back of my mind. I have no idea why, and I'm not sure I like it.

It's true. I seem to have forgotten a lot about the people in the town and their odd mannerisms and behaviours. How did I forget so much? Should I see a doctor about that? Eh, that was a stupid idea, of course I won't do that. Never needed to see them before, certainly not going to start now.

With our guests gone, we carry on sorting

through the boxes. I find myself reminiscing on the past. Since Jill mentioned me being forgetful of the past, I try to think about it. But the more I think of my childhood, the more spots blur. How is it I've forgotten so much? Why is it I've only just realised now, how much I can't remember?

A more startling realisation crosses my mind. I hardly ever mentioned the town I grew up in, whilst I was in the city. Even worse is I never felt compelled to return home, it was always to meet halfway with Jill. Considering my parents were alive for two years after I left, I should have wanted to come back to visit. But I didn't. Christ, I didn't even go to their funeral. Why didn't I go? Thinking back, I can't think of one valid reason for not going. I just know that I didn't even feel a want to go. Loving my parents as much as I did, I should have wanted to go and yet I didn't. Why? Why? WHY?

CHAPTER 4

Strolling into work the next day, my mind is still whirring with questions. The more I think of all the discrepancies, the more my headache blossoms. But it's as though I can't stop myself from fixating on it. As I arrive at the bakery, I get to work rolling out pastry and spooning batter into moulds, I lose myself in the task. Having already gotten into a routine, I find my mind still slipping to all the questions floating about. How is it, even when I arrived, I didn't contemplate how odd it was that I hardly remembered the place I grew up in? I find myself battering the pastry and utensils as my confusion rises.

A clatter pulls me from my musings. In my hand is a metal tray, or at least what used to be a metal tray. Now it's in two halves. How the hell did that happen?

Sue comes rushing in from the other kitchen.

"What happened?" she asks. "Are you alright?" I just stare at the tray in confusion. How does a metal tray break into two? Dent and bend I could understand, but break… "It's alright dear," Sue says softly when she sees what's happened. Gently taking the broken equipment from my hands, she throws it in the bin. Her brow furrows and she bites her lip.

"Sweetie, what's happened over the past couple of days?" she asks softly.

Looking to her I say, "I was unpacking the rest of my stuff yesterday with Jill."

Maybe she's just trying to distract me from what just happened, but I still look to my hands as though the answers to all my questions are there.

"That sounds good," Sue says softly. "What about after you left work the day before? Did you go see your parents and grandparents?" she asks calmly, moving to take desserts out of the ovens and put the next batches in.

"Yea," I answer softly.

As I think to that day, I realise I remember going to the cemetery but not getting home. "How did I get home?" I whisper to myself.

I'd had a blank in the morning, but after everything that happened yesterday, I'd forgot about it. I'd felt like shit when I woke up and just assumed I'd drunk something. Even so, that wouldn't be the reason for me suddenly being able to break a tray in half. Maybe it was old or defective.

"Freyja. Look at me," Sue orders, and the lyrical quality to her voice has me looking up to her. "Go take a break. Calm down. The answers to all your questions will come in time. For now, accept what is, and don't focus on what has been."

For the first time in a day, the tension, that I didn't even realise I had, releases from me. All the stressful events float away on a breeze, and I allow a soft serene smile to spread across my face. If I believed in supernaturals, I'd have said she compelled me. A little chuckle slips out at the thought. Everyone knows the supernatural don't exist.

"You're right," I say, and take myself to get a cup of tea.

For the rest of the morning, I work seamlessly. Baking the sweet treats and preparing batter with ease. I even find myself bopping along to the music Sue put on.

Later on, I'm serving customers while Sue gets some more pastries in the oven. Since Sue calmed me down earlier, I've been able to focus on the task at hand. Obviously, my mind still slips into what happened, but then her calming words float into my mind, and it vanishes.

I don't know what has happened, or when it happened, but I find my eyes straying to the pastries Sue made earlier. They smell divine, and my mouth has been salivating all day. Since starting here, I've smelt the pastries and always look forward to having one, but I've never been entranced by the ones Sue makes. But today, I find my eyes straying to them, and it even seems like I can smell an extra hint of something delicious in them.

In fact, I'm tempted to sneak one of the pastry's home with me. Usually, I just take a couple home from the side I bake, but today I might have to change that. But something warns me not to let Sue see me taking one of those left-over pastries. I've no idea why I shouldn't, but my gut is telling me not to let her see me take them. My gut has never let me down and I doubt it would now.

As the shitty day keeps dragging on, it only gets shitter. The bitch who nearly hit me on my arrival into town, comes strolling in. With her is a god of a man and a group of familiar looking people, two of whom are women and two are men.

The unfamiliar god of a man has slicked-back brown hair and entrancing green eyes. I find my eyes fixating on him. Who is he? And why the hell is the bitch clinging to him? Are they together? Whatever is going on between the pair is none of my business. Or at least it shouldn't be, but my anger flares with how close she is to him. She doesn't deserve him. If it wasn't for the fact, she already has two black eyes, I'd punch her again. But then, I'd be in the wrong and the cops would probably be called, and at least this way the bitch got what she deserved rather than it being me being malicious.

My eyes stray to the rest of the group. Why do I recognise them? It's not from when I was here as a child. It feels like a recent memory, but, as has been happening recently, I can't put my goddamn finger on it. A niggling feeling in my mind is telling me there's a serious reason I recognise them.

With that, Sue's guidance from earlier vanishes, and my anger and stress, returns full force. It barrels into me, and it takes all my effort to keep the faux smile plastered to my face.

"Hello," the entrancing god man greets. "You must be Sue's new hire. It's about time she had help. Although I certainly wasn't expecting such a…"

"Slut," the bitch with him, fills in, with a malicious snarl stretching her botoxified face.

Glaring towards her, I snap, "Coming from you that says a lot. Thought you'd have been arrested by now. Or did you learn your lesson?" I remark.

I delight in the little flinch she gives. Clearly the beating she received is still fresh in her mind.

The guy with her ignores the outburst. "I was going to say, such a doll."

Christ, that's just as bad. If not worse.

"A doll," I screech. "You're a fucking jackass," I curse, letting the irritable mood I've been in all day fuel me.

He rubs me the wrong way and I can't for the life of me figure out why my heart races around him. I should hate the fucker, but that doesn't stop my libido from shooting sky high. God, I want to rub on him like a cat in heat. I growl. Annoyed by my own reactions to the prick.

One of the men I recognise in the group says, "Watch what you say around the..." His words cut off, and he turns ghostly when he sees who he's speaking to. He's wearing a short plaid skirt and rocking it. Seeing the skirt just jolts my memory. I know him.

"Do I know you?" I ask the man in a skirt,

completely forgetting he was complaining at me only a moment ago.

His already pale complexion seems to pale further. "Erm. Errrm," he stutters out. Before he can reply, a pain like nothing I've ever felt before, rips through my skull, and I collapse to the ground. Images flash before my eyes so quickly, I struggle to focus on them.

A cemetery. A deformed gnarled creature. The four people with glowing eyes. Pain. Lots of pain. Then metal. The blissful, painless darkness.

As the images flash through my mind, I scream out. Despite only being memories the pain in them feels all too real. As they continue to flicker in my mind, I push them out. That's all they are, images. It's not real. It didn't happen. Clearly it didn't happen if I'm still alive. Monsters don't exist. Why I think they're memories, I'll never know. But they can't be. They're just odd images, maybe a lucid nightmare, brought on by stress.

After a moment to compose myself, I unsteadily get to my feet. Sue had run out with the scream, and those I was meant to be serving were surrounding me, but I push them away.

"Sorry about that. I don't know what came over me," I chuckle slightly to try and calm everyone's worried glances. It doesn't work.

Honestly, I didn't expect it to.

"Hello, Sir. Could I speak to you in the back for a moment?" Sue asks the hotty with the bitch, but only once I've assured her, I'm alright for the billionth time.

I ignore the impossibility of what had just run through my head. That can't be what actually happened. That's impossible. I'd be dead or in the hospital if that happened. Maybe it was just some sort of waking dream, nothing much. Surely, if I tell myself that enough times, I'll eventually believe it.

I get to work serving the customers.

"What can I get you?" I ask the man in the plaid skirt. I'm sure his name is Hades, but I'm not going to use it. I don't know what I would do if I was right.

"Could I get a croissant and cupcake from the sanguine range please?" he asks.

It doesn't take long to box his items up, and all the while I'm overwhelmed by the gorgeous aroma. What does Sue put in these to make them smell so divine? Wiping my mouth with the back of my arm to check for drool, I try to compose myself. My jaw aches at the thought of biting into one of these goods.

"Here you go," I offer him his cakes.

Once he's paid, he waits to the side for his companions.

As I'm serving the last of his group, the hotty comes strolling out of the back of the shop and offers me a grin as he goes to his friends.

Before he leaves, he looks over his shoulder and says, "I'll be seeing you later, doll." With those promising words, he exits the shop with the four familiar people.

The day drags on and on, until finally it's closing time. I offer to tidy up the front, while Sue gets to work on prep for tomorrow. Whilst she's out of sight, I bag up a couple of treats. One is even from the sanguine side of the cakes. I'm itching to try it, but I should wait until I'm home.

Finally, we close up. I say goodbye to Sue and rush home like a woman on a mission. I suppose in some ways, I am. A mission to devour the sweet treat.

As soon as I'm inside, I open up the box with my goodies. Holding the sweet-smelling treat from the Sanguine range, I take a bite. Instantly, a heavenly taste spreads across my tongue. I accidentally let out a deep groan as my eyes go skyward. These are so delicious.

When the treat is all gone, a deep hunger fills me. The treat filled a little gap, but it wasn't enough. I'm starving, but I don't know what I want. In all my life I've never felt such a deep and wrenching hunger.

Despite all my efforts, nothing I have in the house seems to sate the pit that's opened up in my stomach.

Heading to bed, I toss and turn all night. Not only is hunger gnawing at my insides, but the memories I uncovered earlier are eating me up. It can't be real, can it? I mean, monsters and blood drinking, and dying only to wake up perfectly fine? If I told anyone that, I'd be locked up in a psychiatric facility never to be seen again. For fucks sake. I thought moving back here would be a good fresh start, but it seems more like a nightmare.

CHAPTER 5

What the hell is that fucking noise? Groaning, I pull the blankets over my head, trying, and failing, to block out the sound. It pounds into my skull, threatening to give me a headache. Then again, I could end up with a headache anyway from exhaustion. It feels like I've been asleep for five minutes. The noise doesn't stop. On and on the banging continues.

"Shit," I curse, pushing myself up in bed.

Someone's at the door. How did it take me so long to figure that out? Who in the hell is at my door at this time? Do they know it's considered rude to keep banging on the door when someone hasn't answered?

Rolling out of bed, I blink at the bright lights and make my way downstairs. Unlocking the door, I open it making sure my thoughts on their being at my house is fully understood. Stood there are a man and woman, I remember from the cemetery. Of course, I can't actually remember their names. Too damn tired to figure that shit out.

"What?" I ask sharply. Both of them seem rather unsettled by my snippiness, but I don't give a rat's ass. Who goes knocking on people's door at the butt crack of dawn?

"Erm… Hello ma'am, we're Hades and Harriet," the pink skirt wearing sex god greets. "We've been ordered to come and speak to you today. It seems a concern has been raised that you are in fact transitioning," Hades offers. With one look at the bright pink skirt, I remember which of the group he is. With long brown hair, gorgeous pale brown eyes and a permanent smirk, I know he's the jokester of his friends.

I'm surprised I didn't remember his name from yesterday, but I suppose being woke up so unexpectedly means your brain isn't in full gear.

Harriet on the other hand is a brilliant blonde. Her hair is perfectly straight and secured into a tight ponytail. She's rather short in stature, although the way she holds herself, speaks of confidence and strength. If my memories are to be believed, she's deadlier than she looks. She's also dressed to kill in what appears to be combat gear. A holster straps across her chest and waist, although it's currently free from any weapons at the moment. She looks like she means business and I get the feeling she isn't someone you want to mess with.

Then something else occurs to me. Hades confirmed his name. I'd said it was that but didn't want it to be right. How can I know his name? I didn't actually get attacked in the cemetery. It was obviously just a bad dream, so how the hell do I know his name. Was it just a dream? I couldn't have actually been injured that badly or I'd still be in the hospital, or dead.

Pushing down the fear and confusion, I run through what Hades had said.

"Transition?" I question. "Because I'm new to town? You realise I grew up around here, right?" My brow furrows. I expected odd with Hades, but not downright confusing. What the hell's he on about?

Obviously, I don't actually know the pair. But I seem to be able to get good reads on people, and Hades strikes me as an odd person, but the sort of person who is fair and kind. He reminds me of Loki the God of mischief in the sense he can be a loose cannon, but he isn't malicious. Clearly, I don't know for definite, but that's the impression I get.

Harriot strikes me as level-headed and serious. That's not to say she can't have a laugh and a joke, but she's less for the joking when it comes to business. Whatever business that may be.

Harriet gives Hades a concerned side eye and says, "No, we mean you're transitioning into a supernatural. It would seem there was an incident in the cemetery where you did in fact die, which triggered a supernatural side to come through."

I look at their serious faces and let out a laugh. When they don't join in, my laughter dies off. Are they serious? Surely not. It must be a joke. I expect a joke like that from Hades but not from Harriet. Christ, I'm the one who said Harriet strikes me as level-headed and not one to joke. Maybe my ability to read people isn't working on them because they can't be serious. The supernatural do not exist.

"Riiigghhtt. So, what exactly are you guys here for?" I ask. My decision has been made. I'll placate them until they leave. Then my life will be back to normal. What's the saying... if you can't beat them, join them. Well, I'll pretend to be understanding in whatever they say, and then when they leave, I'll act like it never happened and carry on with my life. Obviously, I just have to blank them for the rest of my life. It'd probably be a blink of their lives since they are supposedly supernatural. Isn't that what they say, that the supernatural have extended lifespans.

"Oh. We're here to inform you of your next steps," Harriet jumps at the opportunity to explain. "We all live at the Estate. You are more than welcome to live there until you get accustomed to your new abilities. We can also provide any food you will need. We suspect you're a vampire so we can provide blood," Harriet offers, in a matter-of-fact tone.

My stomach rumbles loudly. I ignore it. There is no way on Mother Gaia that I like the sound of consuming blood. That's just disgusting. Bloody cuts and injuries, I can deal with. Especially, when it was from me dishing out some well-deserved justice to a prick. But consuming blood... that's a recipe for diseases and illness.

Looking at the serious expressions on Harriet and Hades, I try to figure out just what the hell is going on here. Do they drink blood? Is this some part of a weird cult? They seem to believe every word they're saying, and I can't tell just what brand of crazy they're rocking.

It takes all my will power to not burst out laughing in their face, or run for the phone, claiming there are some people in need of psychiatric assistance. Plus, if I did that, they'd probably kill me for 'attitude'. Or drain me of my blood. Sort of a, can't convince her, so eat her moment.

The part of me that sees logic in what they're saying, I purposefully squash down. I am not losing my mind. Supernaturals aren't real. They never have been, and they never will be. I will not join these mentally unstable people in the hospital.

It's like when a child wishes to be a fairy or to see a unicorn. The parents placate the child by saying that would be lovely, but it's always considered fictional. Now I have two people sat here trying to tell me it's all true. I wouldn't believe them, if not for the fact I have memories of being thrown against a tree by a weird monster. I wouldn't believe them, if not for the fact I knew Hades' name, when the only time I had met him was when I was being thrown against a tree. I shouldn't believe them. But a tiny part of me can see a bit of the logic behind it all.

"Well, you've certainly given me food for thought," I explain, "I'll be sure to think it all over, but right now I need to get ready for work." Despite me believing I'd done a good job of placating them, the side eyes they give one another suggests otherwise. But alas they leave. No more dealing with the crazy people.

The memory of my back crunching around the tree, flashes before my eyes. Sucking in a startled breath at the faux pain, I push it all down. There is no way that could have actually happened. Absolutely not. No way. It doesn't matter that I knew their names. Or that they look familiar. I did not break my spine on a tree. I couldn't have.

But then what sort of sicko dreams something like that up? ... Scratch that, I once dreamt about dead children coming down a conveyor belt in an airport. So, I guess I am sick enough to dream something like that up.

Ignoring the freakiness of the past hour, I get myself ready for work. Despite it being early to go to the bakery, I have a key and figure I might as well make a start, rather than sit around. I'm too antsy to do nothing.

Arriving at work at 10am by myself is odd, since I've grown used to walking in with Sue. But she already said she trusts me with a key and gave me one early on. I'm going to prove that there is a good reason to trust me. After making a drink and putting my things away, I head into the kitchen and start shaping out dough and spooning batter into cases.

"Making an early start today?" Sue enquires, as she comes bustling into the bakery sometime later.

"Sure am." I offer. Then explain, "Some rude people decided to wake me up early for some weird talk. Once I got rid of them, I figured I might as well make a start. I'm not one for sitting idly by when there's work to be done and gorgeous cakes to be made."

She proceeds to collect my mug, whilst pulling her own down from the cupboard. "So, I suppose you didn't put much stock into what they were talking about," she asks as she places a teabag and sugar into each mug.

"Absolutely not," I laugh. "The poor guys seemed to be under the impression that the supernatural are real. Kept going on about me changing and them being able to help. They even mentioned the freaky house on the outskirts of town," I explain. She joins in chuckling. "Get this. They mentioned drinking blood. How barbaric is that?" I say gobsmacked. Sue rolls her eyes, scoffing in disbelief. It eases my frayed nerves to know I wasn't being stupid trusting my mind into not believing them, rather than going with the instincts telling me they were right.

"Well, I certainly wouldn't worry about them," she remarks and with a fresh brew we both crack on with work.

A while later she says, "Have you met the

Sheriff yet?"

"Erm. I'm not really sure who the Sheriff is anymore," I reveal. When I was younger the Sheriff was Jillian's dad. I've not yet seen Jill's mum or dad, so I have no idea if they are still in the area or even if they're still alive.

Why haven't I asked Jillian about her parents? What the hell has happened with my mind, that I've blanked out so much of my childhood here, including the parents of my best friend. Now that I think of it, Jill never bought up her parents. She'd only talk about us and her life while we were together. Sometimes she'd mention her work at the school, but never her parents.

I should probably speak to Jill about that. Maybe even pop over to the house to say hi. I really hope they didn't die while I was away.

The days only just started and already I'm fed up and have had enough. I thought moving back home would be a smart move but so far, I'm regretting it. All the memories and questions that keep popping up are just adding to my confusion, annoyance and the small part of me that feels fear. I say small because not much scares me. Or at least that's what I tell myself.

Pushing all the confusion down, deep into the pit of my mind, I get back to work. Allowing the monotonousness of the tasks to lull my mind and calm me.

Let's just hope things get a bit easier to deal with soon.

CHAPTER 6

The bell chimes as the first customer of the day enters. They're quickly followed by a large line of people waiting for their daily fix of baked goods.

Sue's bakery really is the main meeting group for people. Some towns have a town hall, a library, or other buildings they use as the centre of their town life. Ours is a bakery. People come here every day to get the latest information. They will post any information for the neighbourhood on the bulletin board. They may meet out of towners here, in order to get a read on them before they offer any sort of business proposition. Everyone loves the bakery.

Halfway through the line, I'm finding myself automatically doing things. Setting up the boxes for the baked goods is becoming muscle memory. Remembering where each pastry is, is no longer a problem. Even knowing the prices is becoming easier to remember. One of the regulars who always gets the same pastries doesn't even have to tell me what he wants as I remember it perfectly. He even leaves a tip for being able to remember. I guess it's true what they say, the more you do something the easier it becomes.

"Hello, what can I get for you today?" I ask the next person in line as I get a box ready. When there's no response, I heave out a breath. Please don't let it be one of those difficult customers. Or someone who still hasn't decided what they want, despite having plenty of time to decide.

Looking up, I see the familiar blue eyes and glossy light brown hair. A squeal escapes me as I rush around the counter and run into the arms of Jill's dad, Mark. He embraces me in a tight hug that feels like coming home. It seems I'm not the only one who's happy to see each other again. The hug lasts longer than someone would probably expect, but when you haven't seen someone who you see as a father for years, it's safe to say it will be a drawn-out greeting.

I can't believe how good he looks. He was always well built, and tall. There's an ageless beauty to him. Despite not seeing him for a good few years, he looks exactly the same, and all I can do is stare in awe at the man.

"It's good to see you Trouble," he says softly, with tears rolling down his cheeks.

He holds me at arm's length, taking me in, before embracing me again. The realisation I'll never get to do this with my own father ever again, has me holding onto Mark even tighter. Why didn't I ask about him when I was away? It makes no goddamn sense.

"Why don't you two go out for the day, and get caught up," Sue offers when we are both teary eyed and... you guessed it, still hugging.

Pulling away from Mark, I say, "Oh shit, sorry. And no, no, absolutely not. We will catch up another time." I know how busy it is in the shop and don't want her to have to struggle by herself.

I hate it when people offer things like that. I always feel so guilty. That's another reason me and Jack, my ex, argued so much. He'd call me soft and sensitive. He's the sort of guy who likes to blame things on women's hormones. Still when I have a job, I like to have my work hours and my non-work hours. Niceties are good and all, but you never know if someone will use it all against you one day. I don't like owing people anything.

"Nonsense," She says seriously. "We got even more prepped and ready today as you were here early. Go and catch up. You deserve it," she offers, and after a little more pushing on her end,

I relent and go to collect my things from the back. I'm all but pushed out the door with a promise that she won't hold it against me. That woman is far too good at reading people.

We make our way to Marks squad car, and I let out a chuckle. Once sat in the front and belted up, I turn to Mark. He too has a large grin lighting up his face, showing his dimples.

"I was such a violent child," I laugh.

All those times, he or one of his deputies had handcuffed me, and put me in the back of the car was ridiculous. The only reason I was never locked up, was because after every incident, it was proven that I was only defending someone else. I never started the fight. I ended them. They obviously still had to double check. Even I know being friends with the Sheriff wouldn't protect me if I actually did something wrong. But all the memories of sitting in the back, handcuffed, brings giggles rising up. It's an odd thing to be laughing about, but I became known in the town as the protector. At one point, I even got the nickname Wrath.

When I was older, I was still violent, but I also started to add a dose of sarcasm, or humour, to everything I did. Often when the handcuffs came out, I would reply with, 'Yippee'. At one point a new officer had started working. The other deputies sent him to deal with me as some form of hazing ritual. Anyway, he'd cuffed me, and told me I was going to be punished for my behaviour. I responded with, 'promise'. He'd been so stunned and the deputy with him had nearly pissed himself laughing, knowing full well what I meant.

"We've missed you so much," Mark says, still appearing teary eyed. "What made you come back to town?"

"I'm sorry I didn't come and visit. I've missed you all," I start. Rubbing at my eyes to clear the tears, I add, "But I'm here now, and I'm not going again." Then I debate whether or not to tell him the truth. Knowing how well he can get the truth from people; I figure there's no point lying. I also know he would never use it against me or judge me. "I got a divorce. When I started looking at houses to buy, my family home popped up almost instantly. It seemed like it was meant to be, so I put an offer in... It... It was weird though. Since I've come back, I keep questioning why I didn't visit. It makes no sense to me. I have so much family here. Even without my parents and grandparents, I still have you guys and I still have friends, obviously they were mostly adults but still... why wouldn't I come back?"

He looks to me pursing his lips, "I thought it was because of the incident."

As he drives along, I remember that day. I remember what happened and I find myself, not unbothered, more neutral. It was an awful situation, but it happened a long time ago and I'm over it. I'm not the same person I was back then, and I doubt 'He' is too. Would I be friends with him? Absolutely not. Am I likely to beat the shit out of him? Absolutely. But am I haunted by the incident? No.

"That's what I told people, but I don't understand why," I say. "I'm over it. Even if I wasn't, I'd have still worked up the courage to come to my parents and grandparents' funerals, and yet I didn't have any inclination to do that. It's like it was an out of sight, out of mind, situation."

Mark gives me a guilty expression. It's one that says he knows more on the situation than I do. That being said, I'm not entirely sure what the 'situation' is. Before I have a chance to ask, Mark explains, "I know why. It's difficult to explain, and you're going to think I'm as insane as the two vampires that visited you this morning...." I snort my amusement, but the side eye Mark gives me has me quieting. "Yes, the supernatural are real. The entire town is made up of supernatural beings. However, when you reached adulthood without revealing any supernatural abilities, it was decided the best course of action would be to send you on your way. This was difficult for everyone, but ultimately it was for your protection. This may seem like a quiet town but beneath the shadows of night, it's violent and dangerous."

It takes me a minute to fully comprehend what he's saying. Surely Mark wouldn't play me like this. We've been known to joke around, but he would never play with my head to this extent.

"You were compelled to leave. We also added an element to ensure you wouldn't return unless the compulsion wore off. There's only one reason the compulsion would wear off, and that would be because your supernatural genetics are switching on," he explains. "We were informed about an incident in the cemetery, and it was learnt that you were in fact supernatural, when you lived," he adds, and the memories of that night flash before my eyes.

My gut is telling me he's being truthful, but at the same time believing him means my entire life has been a lie. It means someone forced me away from my home. It means someone forced me to be unable to attend my parents' and grandparents' funerals. Worse, Jillian would have known. Not once did she reveal anything. She knew all this and yet she never told me anything. We told each other everything. Or at least I thought we did.

"So where are we off?" I ask sharply. "I take it you're taking me to the headquarters of the supernaturals or something like that," I add, unable to look him in the eyes.

Anger pours through me at the realisation that I was forced away from my home. Realistically I know Jill was probably under some sort of orders to not reveal anything to me, but I can't help feeling betrayed. Why wouldn't they even come and get me for my parents and grandparents funeral? Allow a reprieve for me to say goodbye to my only family.

But now, I'm finding out it's all because, apparently, the supernatural are real. When I didn't show any 'powers' or whatever they call it, they decided to kick me out. My parents let them, but didn't come with me. Does that mean my family were supernatural? If so, then what were they? Were they vampires, like the two who visited my house, or where they something else?

Shit, do I actually believe Mark? Surely, he's not lying to me. But at the same time, it's just so much to take in, and I still can't ignore that part of me that says the supernatural aren't real.

"Yea, they are friendly," Mark offers, pulling me back into the conversation about those in the supernatural headquarters. Wherever that may be. "They will help you get settled, as well as help you to figure out what you are. The King is also in town, so you will probably be introduced to the community in an event tonight," Mark explains, and I groan at the idea of being forced to interact with a bunch of strangers.

But the more I think about it, the more my interest is piqued. Will there be people there that I know? If this is a supernatural town consisting of mostly supernaturals, that implies there will be those that I know from my childhood. What are they? How many different types of supernatural are there? Who's the King? Who is the King's whore? I remember those in the cemetery discussing this King, and they had mentioned his whore had got into a fight. Will she want to fight me? Oh, I hope so.

Mark glances to me, seeing the grin that's only just lit up my face. "Do not start fights. Supernaturals are made of sturdy stuff. We don't know if you are yet," Mark warns.

Grumbling some unconvincing denial, we lapse into comfortable silence.

CHAPTER 7

We roll up to the creepy estate, and I almost insist that Mark turn the car around. I shouldn't be here. Everyone knows you're not allowed on the estate. It's private property, I'm not meant to be here.

Despite my brain telling me I need to turn around; I also know this is the right thing. This estate is a supernatural meeting ground. Many people stay here. I'm not entirely sure how many people stay on the estate, but from everything Mark's told me there are a lot of people there. It doesn't seem right because from the small part of the estate I've seen, it doesn't look big enough to house as many as Mark insinuated.

Added to the fact every time me and Jill came here as kids, we never saw anybody. Not once. Yet Mark makes it seem as though there are a lot of people who live and work here. How is it possible that we never saw anyone?

Mark scans a badge at the tall swirling gates, and they swing open on silent hinges. We drive in and I hold my breath. My eyes land on the mansion I've seen before. It's still as grand as I remember, only now, ivy crawls across the sides, standing out among the white of the exterior. But as was the case when I was a child, it seems empty. I can't spot anyone inside or around it, and all the windows seem to have curtains shut across them.

I'm surprised when we carry on driving past the mansion. We seem to drive along a smooth road for a few minutes, before finally we pull up to a huge building. Or more accurately, a group of interconnected buildings. Holy shit. Is the mansion on the outskirts of the estate just for show? Is it possible it was used before, but has since been left abandoned? Whatever the case may be, it's clear that that building isn't the main part of this estate, and true to his word, the estate truly is humongous.

It's set out in a horseshoe shape, but even from the main section more buildings seem to sprawl out, with built-in corridors connecting the small buildings to the main. Each one is a different style, showing the era it was made in, and how the area has had to expand over time.

In one word, it's beautiful. Despite it being obvious each building was added in a different period, it still manages to tie in seamlessly to the original building.

I'm that busy gawking at the grandeur, that I don't realise all the people milling about, or how Mark and I seem to have caught everyone's attention. I notice people and some animals, either looking in our direction, or pointing while they talk animatedly. Is it too late to turn back? And what is with those animals? There are predator and prey species living in the same area, without eating one another. Even more freaky, is how they seem to be monitoring Mark and my entrance, as though they too are human. That's not possible right. Animal people?

Mark grabs my hand lending me the strength I need, and we both exit the vehicle. Despite now being able to hear the conversation, I choose to ignore them. What would it matter if they were insulting me? That would just piss me off. If they're complimenting me... ah hell, who am I kidding, it would probably piss me off as well. I'm not the nicest person that's ever lived, as the Bitch learnt on my drive into town. It's probably best I don't tell the King that. He'd probably refuse to acknowledge me or welcome me into the community.

From the little bits I've heard, mainly from

Mark on the drive over, it seems if the King hates you, then you're extremely unlikely to last very long in the community, since the King likes everyone. Those he doesn't like; he has a valid reason not to. Hence why the community also hate them. Best to start on a good note, as opposed to him learning I'm an arsehole with anger issues.

That's another reason I wasn't really up for having kids. My temper is short. I'd agreed to try for kids with my ex, but honestly, I was terrified to fall pregnant. Kids often push people's last buttons, but with how short my fuse is... I'd be a terrible mum.

"Where'd you mind go?" Mark asks, when he notices I'm not paying attention.

Shaking my head, as though the physical action would help to clear my thoughts, I smile and say, "Nothing. What was you saying?"

We both head into the main building as Mark offers an explanation to the purpose of the estate in a magical town.

"Despite folks in town possessing magic, we still get humans here," Mark starts. "In a way this estate is a safe haven. It's also mostly for the royals. When they visit, they live here. It's easier to defend in case of an attack and is protected by wards as well as guards. New supernaturals will often stay here for a few years, until they have control of whatever newfound abilities they have. It protects them and the community. One of the biggest rules is; if you reveal your magic to a human, you will be locked up. It depends on each situation, as to what institute the individual is sent to," he explains.

A shiver works its way through me. The knowledge they have institutes to lock away troublesome supernaturals is both comforting and terrifying. How long will it be before I'm locked away?

"If there are wards protecting the estate. How did I get onto the property as a child?" I ask Mark trying to figure out how this all works. Surely if I was human as a child, I wouldn't have been able to, as it's protected from humans.

"We thought it was because you were magical. It left us confused but hopeful when your powers didn't emerge," he explains. "We hoped that you were just a late bloomer and that your ability to pass through the wards, meant there was magic somewhere inside you."

We head through the entrance, where people, mostly guards if the cargo trousers and smart shirts are anything to go by, walk and talk. The top even has a logo on it reading SGF, with an intricate design of a fiery bird and blood, with some vicious looking weapons including a mace. Some of the inhabitants have obvious weapons attached to their persons, while others look deadly enough to not need them. When they barely even acknowledge me, something inside me rises up. It's as though they think I'm not a threat to them. Not strong enough to beat them in battle, and it sets me off. Despite me always having a temper, this sort of reaction is very new. Pausing, I take a deep breath, trying to push down the feeling of wanting to fight.

The guards closest to me must get the impression something is wrong, as they all maintain a wide berth from me. My skin tingles, and it's as though electricity is coursing through every nerve in my body.

"Freyja, breathe deeply. Remember your anger management training," Mark says, which really doesn't fucking help. This isn't just anger. It's predatory.

Growling, I spit, "Not that fucking simple."

Just as I'm beginning to get very concerned about attacking someone for some unknown reason, a smell hits me. It smells of gingerbread and hot chocolate. All the anger inside me floats away as the scent fills me. Looking down, I spot my two favourite items right under my nose.

"Nice to see that trick still works," Mark

offers, grinning at me.

That sweet tooth I mentioned is serious business. Although I really have no idea how that helped. Or why the scent seems to cocoon me in feelings of safety and security. Then again Mark used to do that a lot. If he saw me getting overwhelmed or too angry to control, he'd bring a hot chocolate and some gingerbread. It wasn't by any means a reward. He wasn't rewarding bad behaviour. It's more that, when my anger rises up, I often can't physically pull myself away. It bombards me until all I see is red. He tried that trick before, and it works surprisingly well to pull me out of the anger.

Munching on the gingerbread, we continue down a hallway. We stop at a little alcove.

"Someone will meet you here, to show you around. I'm really sorry. I wish I could stay, but I've got a call and I'm needed. Will you be alright?" he says.

Nodding my head in an automatic response, he gives me a quick hug and leaves. Part of me regrets telling him I'll be alright by myself, because despite being an independent woman, this entire situation is more overwhelming than I think I can realistically bare.

It isn't long until someone comes waltzing over and I groan at the familiar face. He's tall and lithe, but I can sense the strength behind him. My predator seems to rise up, although unlike last time it seems to be more curious as opposed to hostile. The man stops in front of me, giving me a warm smile.

I don't let the smile fool me. My mind flashes back to the first time I met him, and despite my instincts not encouraging me to fight him, my brain is still insisting I do.

"Hi, Doll," he offers by way of greeting.

"Hello," I offer, covering my mouth until I've finished my bite of food.

The prick may irritate me to the high heavens, but I'm not going to show him all the mushed food in my mouth. That's just disgusting. Even by my standards.

"I'm Xander," he offers. "It's a pleasure to officially meet you...," he trails off, waiting for me to give him my name.

"I'm Freyja. Not Doll," I say tersely. "And I can't say it's a pleasure to meet you. Pretty sure I could have gone my entire life without speaking to you."

"Well, you're beautiful, like a porcelain doll," he explains, with a grin. "Hence why you are, Doll."

"Beautiful?" I ask, giving him a crazed look.

Snorting I say, "I'm a divorcee, so clearly not beautiful enough to keep a marriage."

"Are you sure that's not just because of your charming personality?" he asks, his voice dripping with sarcasm. How can I make every conversation into an argument?

"I'll have you know I have a brilliant personality," I defend. "Mark, Jilly and Eve don't seem to mind it," I add, bringing my second family into it. There has to be a valid reason they like me so much.

"Wait, you don't happen to be the psycho sister Jill is always raving about," he asks. "The one who would repeatedly get arrested, to the point every officer in the station had arrested her at least five times."

"I'll have you know that was always in defence of another," I argue. "There were never any charges pressed."

"Of course, Jailbird. I'll take your word on that," he offers, with a huge grin on his face.

"Jailbird," I scream at him in absolute shock. I can't decide which is worse, Doll or Jailbird.

Before he can reply, one of the guards comes over to him. "Sir, she's insisting she needs you," I hear the guard say to him in a hushed whisper.

"Seriously. It was a black eye. It would have healed by now," he retorts, and my interest is certainly peeked. It would seem he's discussing the bitch I attacked in self-defence. Or at least it certainly sounds like that. I thought the bitch was with the king. Maybe it's not her then. Afterall, there's no reason the King would be talking to me.

More words are muttered, but I don't quite hear them. With a parting smirk, Xander leaves me here, silently wishing he would come back so we can verbally spar some more. He's one hell of a man and I would love to take a bite out of him. Yummy!

Then I curse myself. I will not fall for the arsehole.

It's only once he's disappeared from sight that I curse. Was he meant to show me around the place?

CHAPTER 8

T hankfully, he wasn't in charge of showing me around, and a young woman around my own age comes over to meet me. Her fiery red hair falls straight to her mid back. A bright smile adorns her face, and a spring accompanies her step. She's petite but carries herself with confidence. I've never met a woman so gorgeous. I'm a bit jealous.

"Hi, you must be Freyja," the fiery red head greets. "I'm Alexis, it's lovely to meet you. Jill talks nonstop about you," she chirps, and a few things cross my mind.

The first is that she seems very chatty and innocent. She's going to be in for a surprise with me. The second is that she knows Jill. If Jill truly does know her, and has spoken to her about me, then maybe my foul attitude won't be too surprising. It will be interesting to see whether or not I'll bother her with my foul and dark attitude.

Alexis takes me through the main building, showing me where everything is that I need to know. The King and his entourage stay at the top of the building, also known as the 6th floor, and can be accessed by anyone, but there is an expectation that you only disturb them when necessary. The four upper floors are other people's quarters, although not all supernaturals live there. It's often those who work on the estate or for those new to the supernatural world.

She then explains where everything is located, rather than show me because, in her words, 'you won't use most of that shit'. It's mostly maintenance areas. Another building for the tech geeks, because they have an entire team dedicated to ensuring that word on supernaturals doesn't reach the humans. As well as monitoring the supernatural search engine. It all sounds rather fascinating, although not exactly my topic. It was amazing to learn that supernaturals have their own internet browser, or whatever the proper term is.

When I had commented on the human's beliefs on the supernatural, she had mentioned that that was also the work of the technology section. They purposefully put out inaccurate information usually in the forms of stories or in more modern examples, fan fiction. This means that the humans can still enjoy their beliefs whilst also looking out for entirely the wrong things. It's amazing that they even think about such things.

The rest of the buildings are for various businesses for the supernaturals, and typically only those who need to be in the buildings, are. Honestly, I lost interest with the majority of it. My interest is only piqued as she shows me to the training grounds and, holy shit, it's huge. I'm talking an entire football stadium could fit comfortably inside this one building. How does this even fit on the estate? Just how big is the estate? Is this their magic at work, making the estate seem smaller on the outside than on the inside? Is this like the Tardis technology?

"I worked in security," I say, staring in awe at all those currently training. Supernaturals of all types throw punches, and kick into bags that seem to be able to take a beating. "How do those bags not break?"

"They're reinforced with magic," Alexis explains. "They can take a lot, although they still break far too often," she chuckles. "If security work is something you enjoy, we can always see about you working in the guard force."

I think about that for a second. It's been far too long since I last worked as security, but at the same time, I do really enjoy working at the bakery. It's been strangely perfect. Certainly, I wasn't expecting to enjoy it so much. Would I really want to stop that and move into security?

"Possibly. Truth is I'm unsure whether I'd want to stop working at the bakery. I've been really loving it," I explain.

Maybe it's the pastries I'm truly in love with. But I don't think it is. Sue seems to be an amazing woman who is a pleasure to work with. Despite not usually being a social person, I've also really enjoyed meeting everyone in the town and the bakery seems to be the centre of the town. So, I truly don't think I'd want to stop it. It also wouldn't be fair on Sue if I left so soon after starting, especially since she did take a chance with me.

"We might be able to work out a schedule where you train and work. You might even be able to just train, and only work as a guard when there's a need for reinforcements," she explains.

I have to admit that sounds like a good plan. It'll definitely be worth at least training. Getting some of my anger out on a punching bag will probably be a good idea for everyone's safety.

"That could work," I say smiling at the idea.

Hopefully it will work out.

With the tour over, she shows me to her room, where we sit and chat for a while. I'm surprised how much I get on with her, despite her bubbly and energetic personality. However, during the tour, I did notice a surprising amount of strength, as well as a grace and prowess that speaks of someone who is trained. It's boggling my mind a little bit, as she doesn't strike me as the type. Then again, you can't judge someone from first impressions, not everyone is as they first appear.

Plus, as much as it kills me to admit it, they seem to be telling the truth that supernaturals are real. Which would mean Alexis is one as well. Maybe that side of her is what gives her the strength and prowess most untrained humans wouldn't possess. Maybe it's a standard quality for supernaturals to have.

"Oh, you'll have to come to the party tonight. It's sort of mandatory," Alexis explains, and I inwardly groan. Parties really aren't my thing. Clearly, my emotions show as she continues speaking. "It's not that bad. Basically, the King informs everyone of any news they need to know about. You will be formally introduced and accepted into the community, and then we party. Honestly, it's not as bad as it sounds, and only requires a little ritual that won't hurt all that much. The King is also the hottest person I've ever met. I have no idea what he sees in that whore he sleeps with, but still, he's lovely and it's really not all too bad," she rambles, and it's a task in itself to keep up with her constant talking.

My first thought is that this hot as sin King, can't be as hot as the god of a man I've seen around. The guy who loves to call me Doll and has since moved on to refer to me as Jailbird. There is no way this King is hotter than him. But then I focus on the rest of what Alexis has said.

"Right... What's the dress code for this sort of, not a party, party?" I ask, only partially acknowledging what she's said. Mainly because when someone says it's only slightly painful, what they mean is excruciatingly painful and horrific.

"Ooohh, that's the most exciting part," she squeals clapping her hands. "It's black tie. So, get out your fanciest frocks and get prettied up."

"Huh. You seem to be under the impression I own any... fancy frocks," I deadpan.

Her face drops, and without responding she runs into her walk-in wardrobe. I can hear her mumbling away to herself, and the scrapes of coat hangers' rings through the room. When she finally reappears, she's smothered in lace, silks, and all the fabrics in between. Heaven help me.

I've got a feeling they aren't for her to try on.

"So, I know you're a bit taller than me," she starts, and I look at her 5'4 height. I'm more than a little bit taller at 5'11. "Anyway, these are either full frocks that still have plenty of length, or they're shorter dresses. Get trying them on. We'll find you something," she offers, setting the clothes on the bed and taking a seat beside them. I don't care what I wear, but under no circumstance will it be pink.

"I'm not wearing pink," I state, glaring at the offending items.

She reluctantly removes all the pink dresses, and I pick up the dress on the top of the pile. It's a forest green, floor length ballgown. Alexis looks to me with pleading eyes. I quickly peel off my clothing and put the dress on. It's clear Alexis doesn't mind me changing in front of her, which is good because I really couldn't care less about being modest. The dress doesn't quite reach the ground, and it's far too... puffy, for my style. Removing it and throwing it into a new 'hell no' pile, I try on the next. A red number that's closer to something I would wear, but it has clearly been taken up to suit Alexis' size, which means it looks ridiculous on me.

"Is this really necessary?" I ask Alexis, getting exasperated from this entire ordeal.

Not only have I just learnt supernaturals exist, but now I'm having to get all dressed up to impress some stuck-up King, who apparently likes whores. Alright I've only tried on two dresses, but I've never been the sort of person who likes to try on numerous outfits and make myself look perfect. I'm more on the lane of picking up an item of clothing, sniffing it and as long as it doesn't stink, I'll wear it. I don't even care if it matches the rest of my outfit.

"It is. Stop whining and try on some more," she orders, and my god I didn't expect her to be so bossy.

"What are you?" I ask.

I've no idea if it's considered rude to ask someone what they are, but then again, even if it is I don't really give a rat's ass. How else am I meant to learn?

"A vampire," she answers nonchalantly, flashing her sharp incisors at me.

I'd have thought that some primal reaction would happen, where I would at least be slightly scared, but I'm not. Odd. Isn't that what most people experience? If they witness a predator, unless they are a bigger and badder predator, they get a fight or flight response. I don't feel any of that. Only fascination.

"Cool. Is Jill a supernatural?" I ask.

Surely if she's stayed in this town, she is. But I've never suspected anything was different about her.

"She is. But it's not my place to say what. Her family and the Heathen family are slightly different than most families. Or at least a lot of those within the family are different," she says, but refuses to say more, despite the questions I throw at her.

Heathen family? They have a supernatural family with the same last name as me. That's exciting. I wonder if we're distantly related. It's certainly possible since I was only ever close with my parents and grandparents from my father's side. They never spoke of other family members, even when I would ask. I'd figured there was some big falling out, or maybe our family was just incredibly small, but a thrill of excitement worms through me at the idea that I could possibly have more family, even if they are just distant relatives.

After trying on numerous other dresses, I finally find the perfect one. It's black and orange, and certainly not something I ever thought I would wear. It has an open back and plunging neckline and it certainly shows some skin. The skirt is heavy, but it gives it a nice drape that's not too tight, but not too puffy. Most of the dress is black, but the vibrant orange embellishments make me feel like it's Halloween, which all in all is not a bad thing.

"Wow. That looks perfect on you," Alexis states, looking into the mirror with me. "I can't remember ever seeing it before... huh... it was probably a gift or bought during one of my shopping trips. Either way, it looks as though it was made for you. Keep it. Wear it tonight and start your collection of fancy frocks," she adds with a twinkle of excitement in her eyes.

I snort, "Collection implies I'll be getting more, which I highly doubt. I'm not the dressing up type of person."

"We'll see about that," Alexis says ominously.

Fucking hell, what have I gotten myself into this time?

CHAPTER 9

Standing outside the grand ballroom, I curse Alexis. She told me it was no big deal. She neglected to mention that this was also a welcoming ball. Every supernatural in attendance is there to see me. The new supernatural. This is beyond a joke and the next time I see Alexis she is a dead woman. Although, she's a vampire, doesn't that mean she's already dead? Or is that not the case? I really need to learn more about this new world.

Laughter proceeds my best friend making an appearance. Glaring at the slut, I try to calm my anger. I know for a fact she told Alexis to lie to me about today. Afterall, Alexis and Jillian are good friends, and Jill knows me well enough to give Alexis a heads up. For fucks sake.

The fact I've been told to wait outside the

grand ballroom, speaks volumes about exactly the sort of event this is. I highly doubt it's a common occurrence to have such a formal event for the King to only inform the community of current news. Jill would know how I'd feel about being put on display. So, Jill would have lied to Alexis, so I'd actually show up. I'm really contemplating ripping into Jill. Should I? Or should I just get pay back on a later date?

"You look hot as sin. You should wear fancy frocks more often," Jill offers, smiling sinisterly.

She doesn't give me any time to respond before she heads into the room. I don't manage to see much but the sound of so many people chattering, has me cringing. Socialising on this level makes me want to throw up.

"Don't worry, Jailbird. It won't be that torturous," Xanders voice rings out. Of course, he's got to push all my buttons.

Today he's wearing a lovely black suit, lined with dark blue. It has a matching tie. The trousers hug his backside, and it takes all my effort to not stare. I've got a thing about butts, and his is the most biteable of all the butts I've looked at. Not to toot my own horn, but I've certainly seen a lot. Obviously done so, very discreetly. I'm not like men after all who have no discretion at all.

"It sounds pretty torturous, in fact death by

a thousand cuts sounds more pleasant right now," I offer, ignoring the jailbird comment. "Maybe even being roasted in a brazen bull. Or scaphism. Yeah, that all sound more pleasant than going in there and... socialising," I gag at the end, just so he knows exactly what I think of the damn activity.

"I shouldn't be surprised you know torture methods, should I? Certainly, fits in with you being a jailbird and all," he laughs. I don't.

"Well, it certainly beats being a pompous prick like you. How is your woman with a black eye? Can't she take a punch?" I ask.

"I'd love to know who did that to Karen. Supernaturals heal quicker than most and it's worrying that she hasn't healed yet. Nothing should be able to do that," he explains, and it certainly piques my interest. Supernaturals heal quicker and I'm assuming bruises should heal quite quickly, but I need to research more before making any assumptions.

Although just as he would like to know who did it, I'd love to know too. Is it the same woman I punched. If so, who punched the kings whore? Maybe there's someone here I'd actually get along with. We could spar sometime and compare notes.

Snorting I say, "Her name's Karen? Well, that explains why she got beat up."

He quirks his eyebrow at me, and I smile brightly. "Right. Maybe don't make assumptions about people before you meet them. She's not that bad," he explains seriously, and I still chuckle.

Maybe he's right. But something tells me he's currently thinking with his cock rather than his actual head.

"I'll just have to take your word on it. I suppose it could be worse. Apparently, the supernatural King is dating a whore." I all out belly laugh. "She seems to be quite the arsehole if everything I've heard is to be believed." I add smiling brightly. He smiles back, nodding his head and quirking his brows again. That's the look of someone who knows something I don't. Ah, well. Who cares! I'm sure I'll catch on soon.

"I'll see you in there, Jailbird," he winks before leaving me alone, yet again, outside the huge doors.

Not too long after, a couple of the King's guards come out of the ballroom to collect me. They have plain black suits on with the same emblem on them of SGF with weapons, blood and that same fiery bird. They don't however wear a tie, likely as that could be seen as a choking hazard if a fight was to break out. It probably wouldn't kill a supernatural, if their strengths are true, but it could potentially distract them enough for a killing blow to be dealt. Heaving a long dramatic sigh, I follow them in. The large crowd parts as I make my way through, until eventually the crowd parts to show the supernatural King and his mistress.

A little squeak escapes me. This isn't going to end well. The King, Xander, smirks at me. The bastard didn't bother telling me who he is. For fucks sake. Honestly though, he's the least of my problems.

"You bitch," the King's mistress shrieks at me, and I wince at the pitch, my guess is she's a banshee if she can reach that eardrum bursting pitch. "This is the bitch who attacked me. I want her arrested immediately," she adds.

I inwardly groan at the idea of being arrested yet again. I've gone years without a single incident, but a few days back in my hometown and I'm at risk of getting arrested again. Surprisingly, no one moves.

"Miss Smith, would you care to address the accusation of you attacking Karen McCloud," the King asks.

I look around trying to ignore the curious gazes. It's rather intimidating to have hundreds of pairs of eyes watching you so intently. Even more so, when your best friend is glaring at you, with a 'tell me you didn't' expression. Also don't ask how that can be an expression because I don't even know, but her look says that exact thing. Or maybe it's just because I know her so well. Still, I look back towards the King and give a confident bravado. Afterall, I wouldn't say I was in the wrong for what I did. Alright it was possibly a violent reaction, that may be considered extreme, but ultimately, she got exactly what was coming to her.

"Sure, I attacked her, but she started it. After nearly hitting me whilst speeding, the bitch decided to rip into me, for nearly scratching the paint on her car. Then she proceeded to pull my hair, which as you can imagine reflexes kicked in, so she got an elbow to the gut. She thought it would then be a good idea to trip me, so she learnt her lesson," I explain calmly, and not at all bothered by the idea I could be in trouble. Sure, I shouldn't have punched her and blah blah blah. But at the end of the day, she did start it. I simply finished it. The question is whether or not the King believes me.

"Fascinating. That adds up a lot more than what you said," the King looks to his mistress giving her a death glare. Ooh. The bitch is in trouble. "Please remove Karen McCloud from the room and put her in the cells until I can discuss this issue with her. I do not tolerate dangerous driving, nor do I condone such blatant rudeness and violence when it is uncalled for," he says much to everyone's amusement. I can't tell, if it's because I also got really violent, and I'm not being removed. Or if it's because they were all excited to see her get what she deserves. "Also dear," Xander adds turning to Karen, "our partnership will not be continuing."

The blonde-haired bitch is dragged from the room kicking and screaming. When a cheer starts up, I can't help the grin that spreads across my face. Eventually the King quietens everyone down by simply raising his hand.

"Well, welcome to the supernatural estate. Here you will learn all about your new side and abilities," the King greets. "Now in order for you to connect with those of the estate, there's a little ritual that has to take place. Don't worry, it doesn't hurt much."

Why does everyone keep saying that? I wouldn't be panicking that it was painful if people didn't bring it up. Most of the time, people only say it won't be too painful, when it's actually horrendous. I swear it's some fucked up method of making people buck up and shut up. Almost as though, if you find it painful, you're a weak little shit. If anyone knows me at all, they know I will refuse to be considered a weak little shit.

"Alexis, Rosemary and Elana please come

forward," he orders, and the three women step forward. "Alexis will bite you to stun your body into staying still. Rosemary and Elana are witches who will perform the spell needed to unite you with the rest of the estate. Do you consent?" the King asks me.

Does he honestly think I'll shy away from it? I'm a badass and that's not me being narcissistic, that's me being truthful. It's like me saying I have zero social skills, it's not me putting myself down, it's me being honest. I don't know how I feel with being connected to those of the estate, but I suspect it's more so that urgent information can be given with ease, sort of like a phone. Why they can't just use technology is beyond me, but I'm sure they have their reasons.

"Sure. Go ahead," I say.

Facing the King, Alexis stands behind me, tipping my neck to the side. Rosemary and Elana step in front of me, holding tightly to my hands. They start building their magic up, and the electricity in the air has my hairs standing on end. If I didn't believe in magic before, I sure do now. Especially as purples and blues start glimmering around their hands. Alexis pierces my neck, and my eyes roll to the back of my head. However, it's not from pain. Pleasure fills every inch of my body; unlike anything I've ever felt before.

Electricity and fire burn through my body, but it weaves with the pleasure until I'm shaking with need. It's more intense than any orgasm I've ever had, and I drift in the pleasure, oblivious to those around me. When the magic stops, Alexis frees her fangs from my neck. I'm thankful she doesn't let me go because I would fall to the floor in a puddle. God, I need a date with Vivian asap.

"You did not tell me it was like that, Alexis. You said painful. I was expecting painful," I snarl softly to Alexis, who I thought was becoming a fast friend.

"It usually is painful. No one has ever reacted like that," she offers and the hint of laughter in her voice has me grinding my teeth.

I'm thankful I was facing the King as it stopped the entire room seeing it. The smirk the bastard wears, tells me he knows exactly what happened. When his eyes jump down, I follow his gaze. I curse when I see what's caught his attention. My nipples are poking right through the material. It's thick fucking material, but the fucking things are rock solid.

Didn't someone say something about supernaturals having better senses than humans? Or was it in fiction books I've read? Either way, I really hope that wasn't true, and if it is, that there is too much going on in this

MOLLIE SYKES

one room, for everyone to know exactly what just happened to me. If they know, I'll probably be the biggest freak in the estate and in a room full of supernaturals, that really does mean a hell of a lot.

CHAPTER 10

G rabbing a hold of my bag, I sling it over my shoulder without care.

"Remind me again why I'm shopping with you lot?" I ask, scowling at Jill, Alexis, Rosemary and Elana.

Since we met a couple of days ago, during the ceremony, Rosemary and Elana have joined our little group. Although it's not as little anymore. They seem to be genuine and kind people, thankfully they're not as soft as they look. Their senses of humour are something else, and they know how my special brand of bitchiness works, so don't seem to get too offended. Something tells me that's especially thanks to Jill.

"Because you love us. Also, because you've yet to visit the underground market," Elana offers, quirking her brow. Elana and I are similar in nature. She's more socially awkward than the others and that in itself helped us click. But she has her downsides. For example, she likes to shop. I'm trying to figure out if this will break the friendship. It's a serious thing.

"What's the underground market? Honestly it sounds like the sort of place you'd buy organs from," I remark. When none of them disagree, I pause. "They sell organs?"

"Not human ones. Just animal ones," Rosemary offers.

"The underground market sells all things magical. Including ingredients needed for certain spells, hence the organs. But for the most part you have to order them. It saves on waste," Jill explains.

Part of me is still horrified they would use organs at all. Then I remind myself that even I eat meat and I suppose using the organs in spells actually reduces the waste. The fact they also think about waste and order the organs in to suit their requests makes me feel less icky about the entire situation.

When we head towards Sue's Sanguine Sweets, I balk. Why are we here? Surely there's not an entrance to some top-secret marketplace here. I've never seen it.

Alexis grins at me when she sees my

confusion. "This entrance was closed when you started working here. We had a feeling it would be temporary, but we couldn't reveal it to a human," Alexis explains, and I nod my head, as though I understand. I don't understand.

We enter the bakery, and I breathe in the scent of fresh baked goods. Sue recently took on another part time employee. It was decided, I not only needed time to settle, but it would be beneficial for me to be able to train. So now I work part time at the bakery and Sue still has the help she needs. It also means she can take on even more orders as she has the extra support. There's even talk of doing delivery. The plan is to set up a website. Although we're still working on how to secure it, so only those of the supernatural persuasion can order the baked goods. I suppose that's also, in part, the reason why it's so important to have the technology area of the estate. They would be able to support Sue and help get her website sorted for her. At least I think they'd be able to.

"Freyja, it's good to see you again. I heard you had a rather exciting time at the party," Sue offers. With a quirked brow, I glare at my new friends. "Oh, don't worry my dear. All will make sense sooner or later. Now, you and the troublemakers get shopping. I expect to see many bags when you come back up," Sue orders.

I was hoping we'd buy the baked goods first, but Sue promised to make sure we had plenty to leave with once we were finished. With that promise in hand me and my newfound friends head to a brick wall. How is this a door?

Rolling her eyes at my newness, Jill places her hand on said blank wall and whispers a word. Before my very eyes, a door pops open, leading to a set of steps going down. How is this even possible? Oh, wait, magic. Always fucking magic.

We all make our way down the rather wide staircase. It seems to go on for way too long, but eventually we reach the bottom, and my jaw just about hits the floor. Lining the walls on either side, are stalls filled to the brim with just about all you can think of. From crystals and tarot cards to potions and elixirs. No, I don't know the difference between the two, but the signs clearly state them as two separate items. It's all rather overwhelming and despite not liking to shop, even I find myself slightly excited to explore. It's probably thanks to the newness of it.

We start making our way to some of the stalls. Since I have no idea what I am yet, I have no idea if I'll require certain items to help in any magic performed. So, all the items designed to assist in any sort of spellcasting, I ignore. As we go along, Rose and Elana inform me on what items are designed for witch's spells, so I don't make a complete fool of myself.

Rosemary and Elana are both witches so they would know. Although they don't seem to be interested in any items for assisting spell craft.

"At what point would someone need these," I ask, picking up some random bottle. It's a greyish powder with a picture on the label rather than words.

"Firstly, none of us would need that. It's for men. To help in the bedroom," Rosemary explains taking the bottle from my hands and placing it back on the table.

"Magical Viagra?" I ask. Kind of surprised they would need a magical version.

"Not quite. It doesn't help getting it up, but it does help in other departments. I recommend getting that when you've got a partner. You'll thank me for it," Elana adds, winking at me.

I get the feeling one, or more, of her partners has used the stuff and she was pleased with the results. I know for definite that's the case when a deep blush spreads across her pale cheeks.

"Secondly, items to assist in spell casting aren't needed for all witches or spellcasters. A lot of the time the items merely help channel your magic. If you have enough natural magic and plenty of practice, you don't need them. Hence why we don't buy this stuff. We don't need it," Elana explains. It would seem the supernatural are more complicated than I originally thought. "An easier way to think of it is that witches are weaker magic users. Mages is the term we use for those with enough natural magic to spell cast without the assistance of extra items. Technically me and Rose are Mages."

We carry on exploring the stalls, and I delight in hounding the girls with questions about this new life I'm living. Each time we stop at something I don't understand, they'll patiently tell me all about it, explaining the details I need to understand. It's lucky the roles aren't reversed, because if I was in their shoes, having to stop and explain things, they likely know by heart, I'd probably get irritated and walk off. I'm not the most patient of people.

I buy a new infinity bag. It costs me a large chunk of change, but I'm not going to complain at having a bag that can hold an unknowable amount, without me actually feeling the weight of what's in it. I also buy a keychain with a gemstone cut into the shape of a Pegasus. I'm not sure what it is about the cute little item, but it draws me in, and I couldn't leave without it. The girls gave me odd looks at the purchase, but they kept their mouths shut. Even now, I find myself transfixed by the object and hold it in my hand lovingly, rather than putting it in my bag.

We eventually stop at a little café to take a break and grab a drink. All of us have bought a lot of stuff, but they're the ones responsible for me buying so much. Like the potion that apparently removes unwanted hair for an entire year. It gets rid of leg hair and arm hair without me needing to shave, for an entire year. The girls apparently swear by it. They also loaded me up with chimes and decorations all which supposedly have some magical aspect or another. If it wasn't for the fact the items came in my colours, black, dark blue and deep purple, I definitely would not have bought them. That being said, even I can see the good in owning these objects.

After our drinks we get up and head in the direction of Lonnie's Little Pleasures. The girls practically drag me there. Clearly, it's a favourite of theres. When the woman behind the counter sees them, she gives them a big grin and comes around to give each of the girls a hug. She goes to hug me, but I step back. Contact with people is not something I care for.

"So, this is Lonnie. She makes products designed for pleasure," Alex squeals.

Now I understand their fascination with this stall. I suspect I'll be adding many items to my draw of debauchery, although at the rate this is going, I might need to allocate another draw for all my toys. I look to the table searching all the products. Most are creams or gels designed to magically enhance pleasure. There are even some potions that I have no idea about.

"You need to try this," Rosemary starts, holding up a tin of cream. "You put it on your boobs, and they balloon in size and sensitivity, they even cause lactation. Only for a short time, but for that short time you feel like a hucow. It's amazing," she explains.

I'm learning far too much about the girl's sexual fantasies, and being the twisted person I am, I'm not sure whether that bothers me or not. It's also good to know I'm not the only one who's fascinated by stories on hucow's. Although if anyone ever asks me about it, I will deny, deny, deny.

Still, we carry on perusing the stall, and even I have to admit this stall seems like it's going to become a fast favourite. I pick up a few of the creams and gels. I'm the adventurous kind, so I even add the cream that Rosemary likes so much. I've experimented a lot with pleasure devices and creams before, but none of them have had magical qualities like these ones. None were able to change the fundamentals of the body for purely sexual pleasure reasons. For some that might be scary, but I'm not too worried. As Rose was explaining earlier, nearly all spells have a reversal spell for it. If anything was to go a little wrong, there would be someone who could fix it.

"You need this one," Jill orders, handing me a pink bottle.

"What is it?" I ask, holding the bottle as though it could blow up at any moment.

"It's a libido enhancer. Basically, you take it, and it enhances your horny levels. Takes your orgasms from 10 to about 50. It's amazing. Trust us," she explains. "The first time I used it, I passed out my orgasm was that intense," she adds, oversharing like so often happens.

I kind of want to say, 'I don't need any enhancement in that area,' but I also don't mind the idea of a better experience. There's no harm in trying. Wait...

"There isn't any ... side effects, is there?" I ask.

"Nope. Well, other than some extreme exhaustion after. But ten back-to-back orgasms will do that to anyone," Alexis offers with a broad smile. It would seem there is another oversharer in the group.

I can't fault that logic. Accepting that I'm not going to be leaving without one, I add it to my pile of goodies. After paying we head off to the next stall.

This next stall holds weapons. My eyes light up at the sight. Despite humans loving to use guns, and I am trained in using them; I've also loved learning to use all different weapons. I once tried using a sword, but that went terribly. Archery on the other hand was somewhat successful. My favourite was always the mace, although that tends to be frowned upon. The other girls go to move on from the stall, but I stop, gazing mesmerized at a pair of Maces. They're simplistic but elegant, and the deep blue gem fused into the handle's, glitter in the light. Just like what happened with the Pegasus keychain, I find myself unable to look away.

"How much?" I ask the seller. After being given the price, I debate. It's a lot of money but after a close, thorough inspection I can tell they are incredibly well made, and I would hazard a guess that they're new. Never been used before. In the end, I buy them. As soon as they're officially mine, something inside me fizzles. As though the weapons are connecting with my soul. I refuse to lose these.

"How fascinating," the seller says, staring at the maces in my hand. "They're connected to you. You'll find that you'll never lose them. They will always come back to you," she explains, and I feel the truth of her words. I've no idea how I know it, but deep down I know what she said is true. "Maces don't typically come in pairs due to the weight, but if they've connected to you, it's likely you'll be able to wield both at the same time."

The girls all watch in fascination, as I bond with the weapons.

Eventually, we head back up to the bakery. Before heading home, we buy some baked goods and just as Sue had promised, we had a range of goods to choose from. By the time we had picked out our favourites, even more had been added as Sue chose to treat us all. How she makes any money with all the freebies she gives us is beyond me.

Finally, the day draws to a close and we all head our separate ways. I can't wait to get home and try some of my new purchases.

CHAPTER 11

In one hand I clutch Vivian. My amazingly powerful vibrator. In the other hand is the pink horny potion. Why do I even listen to my friends? Oh, right. Me and sex basically go hand in hand, so I was actually listening to my libido. God that's a bad idea. It always gets me in trouble.

Part of me still thinks this is a bad idea. I mean surely a potion designed to increase libido as much as this one is said to, could be rather dangerous. I'm certain ten orgasms in one night could lead to... I don't even know what it could lead to. But in my mind, I get the impression it would be like a couch potato running a marathon, without any preparation. They'd end up passed out, and probably in hospital. Although, if I ended up in hospital because I'd have had so many orgasms I'd passed out, it maybe wouldn't be such a bad thing. It'd definitely be a story to tell my friends.

Downing the pink shimmering liquid, I cringe at the taste. A mixture of coffee, eggs, and what I'm pretty sure is prunes. Not exactly a pleasant concoction. Magic spreads throughout my body and a shiver races down me.

I've no idea how long it's meant to take to kick in. So, I decide to check the little leaflet that comes with it. I probably should have checked it first, but where's the fun in that. According to this, it's a pretty instant reaction. I don't feel very horny. Other than the race of magic that I first experienced, there hasn't been any noticeable change.

"Urghh, again. Girl, you need a life," someone says. In an instant, I'm on high alert. I'm pretty sure that adrenaline rush has ruined any potential 'me time'. Holding Vivian out, as though it's a weapon rather than a vibrator, I search my room for intruders. When I find none, I listen closely for any sound. "Bitch, I ain't no weapon. You look like a right nitwit now," the voice says again, and something in the words confuses me.

She's not a weapon. Why would she say that? Looking down at my hands, I stare at the vibrator. It stares back. I blink. It blinks. A scream tears from me, when my brain catches up to the fact my vibrator has eyes. Dropping it to the ground, I stare at it. What the actual fuck is going on?

"Dude! Don't just drop me. How would you like it if you were just dropped on your head. It fucking hurts," it calls out to me, and I squeak.

Since when do sex toys have eyes. Why the hell is it talking? What in the seven levels of hell is going on? Did the girls trick me into downing a potion that somehow creates talking sex toys. If they did, I'm going to wring their fucking necks.

"You're talking..." I state.

"No shit," It curses at me. I am being reamed out.... bad choice of words. I'm being berated by a sex toy. What the actual fuck?

"I'm losing it. I'm honestly losing it," I mutter to myself.

Jack always said I was batshit crazy. Maybe he was right. Christ, now I'm thinking my ex was right. Could this day get any worse? I was meant to be having multiple mind-blowing orgasms, and possibly needing hospitalisation for them. Instead, my favourite sex toy is talking to me, and I'm thinking my ex was right. This is so fucking wrong.

Pulling on my big girl panties, not literally,

since I hadn't even undressed yet. I go towards my vibrator, that is cackling like a fricking hyena. Slowly, I scoop up Vivian, holding her at arm's length, and make my way to my drawer. Opening it, I go to lower her down next to all my other toys.

"Don't you dare. I don't want to be near Damien. He's an absolute dick," Vivian offers, and I have to snort at her choice of words.

"Yes. He's a dildo. It's self-explanatory," I remark.

When my other toys start to join in the conversation, I realise this shit is worse than I thought. Throwing Vivian into the draw, and slamming it closed, I grab my bag and shoes before running out the door.

If my sex toys can talk to me, I'll never be able to masturbate with them again. It'd just be too weird. Imagine having a sex toy getting angry at you for wanting to use it. Or worse they could love it, and I could hear a muffled squeal of delight coming from my vagina. Or worse, I could have Barry up my arse, and he could start talking in public. Even if no one else heard him speak, I'd be the one squealing and going bright red in mortification.

I fire off a quick text, telling the girls to meet me at the estate. Then I take the quickest run of my life, making it to the estate in record time. I'm barely even winded when I arrive, which is a miracle in itself. As much as I've always been able to fight, and do so for extended periods of time, when it comes to running, I'm usually useless.

"Where are you, you hussies," I call out, as soon as I'm inside.

Everyone stares at me. Some jump in fright, some going on guard. Ignoring the curious glances, I search for my friends. Heading down the hallway and up the stairs, while people move quickly out of my way. Seems they can sense I'm a hairsbreadth away from ripping someone to pieces. It takes me a few minutes, but I track them down to Alexis' room. Slamming the door shut, I heave in an annoyed breath.

"A potion to increase libido?" I ask. "Are you sure about that?"

The girls look at me like I've gone mad.

"Wait, you already tried it?" Rosemary asks, sounding worried.

"Yes," I state.

"We told you not to practice or consume any magic until the ceremony spell has stabilised. Theres too much rampant magic inside you for potions to take effect," she adds.

My   brain   moves   through   every conversation we've had since that day, and I come up empty. "No, you didn't," I scream.

"I did," she insists.

"You didn't."

She pauses for a moment. Letting out a little chuckle, she says, "Whoops. I meant to tell you that. But in my defence, you orgasmed during a painful ceremony, so I was distracted."

She forgot. Something as serious as that and she forgot to fucking tell me. Not even a reminder, when I bought the damn thing. Is she crazy? I'm going to kill her. Rose may be sweet and shy, but that doesn't change the fact I'm going to wring her bloody neck.

Alexis looks at me with a quirked brow and pursed lips. "What happened when you took the libido potion?" she asks.

Her question provides Rose with a few more minutes to live.

"You really want to know," I ask.

All four girls have big grins on their faces, like this is the most exciting thing to happen to them. I go quiet, listening to all that's going on in the room. Crouching down, I lift the duvet up to get a peek under Alexis' bed. I spot the box I'm looking for and pull it out.

"Don't go in there. It's private," Alexis

warns, her cheeks flushing.

"I know. But they're screaming about something," I explain, and the grins in the room turn to frowns.

Opening the box, I raise my eyebrow. Lifting out the one item that immediately caught my attention, I give Alexis a questioning look. She just scowls at Jill, who has the biggest shit eating grin on her face. Right, Jill gifted a mega dong to Alexis. I look down at the dildo. It looks back. It's huge. I'm talking feet long rather than inches, and don't even get me started on the girth of the thing.

"So, give me your name and tell me something about Alexis and you," I order the inanimate object.

"Hi gorgeous. I'm Melvin," it says, wearing a dopey grin.

"Melvin?" I splutter, and Alexis' eyes go wide and serious.

"Yep. Did you know she's used me before. She likes to make out she just doesn't know how to get rid of me, but she secretly loves me," he says, still with a big grin. "I love her too," he adds, and I'm speechless.

How the hell does something like that, even fit anywhere? Surely, she's never managed to get the entire thing inside. Crap, now I'm wondering how the hell it's possible.

"Well," I say in utter surprise.

Something tells me I shouldn't reveal Alexis' dirty secrets to everyone, but I just can't believe it myself. Part of me would love to reveal it. To be a true bitch, but really Alexis just bit me. She's not the one responsible for withholding information that could have avoided this entire situation.

"I have so many questions, but I'm too scared of the answer," I remark. Alexis blushes beet red and that seems to clear up everything.

"It's not as difficult as you'd think," she whispers to me, and it's my turn to gawk at her.

"You can talk to sex toys?" Jill asks. When I nod my head, she stands up. "Right, well I've got to go and sort something out. Catch you all later?"

She opens the door and walks out. "Hide your sex toys everyone, unless you want your dirty secrets revealed," she hollers down the hallway, and I can't help the laughter.

I head towards the door, with the dildo still in my hand. Shouting down the hallway, I say, "It's more uncomfortable for me, than it is for you."

Jill looks back. A huge grin lights up her features, as her eyes look to someone past me.

Following her gaze, I turn, finding Xander. Whelp. Apparently, this day can indeed get worse. He's attempting, very poorly I should add, not to laugh. The tears tracking down his cheeks don't exactly hide the fact he's amused.

"If it's uncomfortable, why do you have it?" he asks. Jill's cackle rings down the hallway. I could smack her.

"I wasn't talking about this being uncomfortable," I state.

His eyes go wide. "Something that big, is comfortable?"

Smacking my head into my hand and ending up with a dildo to the face, just about destroys me. By this point, so much blood has rushed to my face in embarrassment, that I'm pretty certain I'm going to drop dead. Instead of multiple orgasms hospitalising me, embarrassment is going to do it instead.

"I'm going to leave before I dig this hole any deeper," I mutter.

Only realising I shouldn't have said anything after the fact.

It's only clarified when Xander states, "It would seem your hole is deep enough already!"

An all-out donkey laugh comes from Jill, as she almost chokes herself laughing so hard.

Worse she isn't the only one. Xander is just as bad. As are my friends in the room. I fucking hate the lot of them.

I march back into Alexis' room leaving Xander outside laughing. After slamming the door closed, I lock it to prevent interruption, and glare at the three remaining friends in the room. Although friends might be a stretch. I currently think they'd be more accurately described as being my worst enemies.

Looking to Rosemary and Elana, I ask, "How can I fix this?"

They converse in glances, and I know it's not good news. "Well, I've never even heard of a potion that can do that. The fact it's a morphed spell anyway, means that it can't be fixed," Rosemary reveals, and I wilt. For fucks sake.

"So, you're telling me, I just have to put up with talking sex objects for the rest of my life?"   I ask. If someone had asked me before I had this 'ability', whether I'd want to talk to sex objects, I'd have thought it was a great idea. Your vibrator being able to discuss ideas and other ways to use it, should be good. But then I'd think about it realistically. It's not a good idea for your vibrator to be able to berate you and curse you off. It certainly doesn't create an atmosphere for play time.

"I thought you said spells have counter spells for them," I state. The only reason I was comfortable drinking the potion down, was because she said they'd be able to counter anything that happened.

"I said, most, have counter spells. Morphed spells aren't something you want to play around with," she explains.

I'm totally screwed. Not literally!

CHAPTER 12

My mind is in a jumble as I head from the estate. It doesn't seem like a big deal, that I can talk to sex toys, but it's not exactly a power I ever wanted. Then again it could be worse. Still, with how new I am to the supernatural world, it's all a little overwhelming.

It doesn't make things any easier, that Xander thinks Melvin is mine. Don't get me wrong, I have some extreme toys, but certainly not anything as big as Melvin. Still, I'm mortified he saw that entire situation. I've never been one to get so flustered, but for some reason around him, I am. It's like my mind is running that quickly, I'm unable to say anything logical and end up making an extreme tit of myself. That's probably half the reason I love ripping into him so much, to hide how uncomfortable I am with the feelings he invokes in me. Mainly, the extreme lust, that always bubbles to the surface.

With a deep breath, I pull myself from my thoughts. Taking in the evening, I smile brightly. Despite the darkness of the night, I can see incredibly well. The trees sway gently in the breeze. The scent of rain on the horizon fills the air. Animals of all kinds chitter and howl. This isn't something you'd experience in the cities.

I missed this when I was in the city. In the city there was never any peace. Too many cars would be rushing by. Too many people talking and bustling by, busy getting from one place to the next. Here it's not like that. People take in the environment around them. We have houses, but we work to ensure to harmonise with the earth. There are cars, but since arriving, I haven't used it. Afterall, it's easy enough to get from one place to the next by walking, unless you're going to the estate. The only reason I ran last time was because I was so worked up.

Being back in this wonderful town, I realise everything I was missing. For the life of me I can't figure out why I would have left. Alright after the incident I was pretty shook up, but I can't figure out why I'd have wanted to leave. It's as though someone else influenced me into leaving and forgetting all about the town.

Again, I have to pull myself away from the dark thoughts. Just because it's difficult settling in, it doesn't mean this was a bad idea. Quite the opposite is true. I love it here. I'm more at peace, and content, than I have been in years. Even when I first got with Jack, I wasn't this happy and at peace. This was a brilliant decision. It's just come with some complications that I have to work through. But I will get there.

"I will get through this," I say to myself out loud.

Halfway home the hairs on the back of my neck prickle, and a rush of anxiety races through me. Glancing around, I search for the cause of my unease. When I don't spot anyone, I carry on my walk. Only the feeling doesn't leave. The more I walk, the antsier I get. Again, I search the area but don't spot anyone. So instead, I look for any businesses down the street. My hope is that I can take shelter in one if needs be. But considering how close we are to the forest, there are only houses and all seem to be vacant, likely with their inhabitants still at work.

I'm not one to be overly dramatic about danger. Nor am I usually so affected by the thought of being in danger. With all the experience I have, very little actually bothers me. But whatever it is that is setting me so on edge, is dangerous. Beyond anything I've ever encountered. I'm almost certain of it.

Listening for any noise, I don't hear anything. In fact, what's even odder is the birds I heard not too long ago, have gone silent. It's as though the entire area has had all the sound sucked out of it. As though the wildlife has also sensed the danger and run from it. Surely if predators are scared of the danger lurking, then it must be bad.

Picking up my pace, I keep my head on a swivel, attempting to discreetly search my surroundings in hopes of spotting the cause of my unease. By this point, I pretty much want to run for my life, but my instincts are telling me that running wouldn't be recommended. Running would be something that could get me killed.

Unfortunately, I don't spot it before something large slams into me with a loud bellow. I land unceremoniously in a heap on the ground, jolting my back and arm in the process.

Blinking away my surprise, I jump to my feet, instantly going on high alert. Despite just being tackled, I don't immediately see my attacker. When I do, the blood drains from my face. Stood a few feet away is a monstrous creature towering over me. With a ghostly appearance that's also somehow solid, and large mangled appendages, it's a sight I'll never forget. It's also a sight that's far too familiar.

The cemetery. It's the creature that attacked me in the cemetery.

If my memory is right, it took all four of those supernaturals to kill that monster, and here I am with nothing but pepper spray and a multi-tool. I'm dead. A cold chill races through me, and for the first time in my life I have the urge to flee from the danger.

Still, I pull on my big girl panties and prepare to fight, knowing that even though my urges are telling me to flee, that wouldn't be a good idea. The creature circles me, and I maintain sight with it at all times. Despite the creature circling me, the hair on my neck prickles. I'm still being watched. Please don't tell me there's more than one.

The creature in front of me charges. I swipe out with my multi-tool as I step out of its way. Its once cautious attack turns rabid. It seems to attack from all angles. Claws swipe at my sides, and I hiss in a breath.

"Fucking prick," I curse, slashing, punching, and kicking with all my might.

Spraying the pepper spray towards its eyes, it bellows. Using its distraction to my advantage, I stab towards its throat, happy when a spray of something comes from it. Is it blood? It's black and smells worse than a dead body. Gross. Still, I jab at it again and again, hoping to kill the damn thing.

It doesn't die, and eventually it swipes at me again, sending me soaring. I land in the middle of the road with a thud. My head hits the pavement. Stars dance in my eyes, but I blink them away.

Whatever that creature is, it's got some immense strength and I'm really starting to think I'm going to die here. Again, if my death in the cemetery was real.

"Here," someone says, handing me a weapon. A mace.

I'm so surprised to see someone else there, that I'm momentarily stunned. Christ this new life is really throwing me for a loop. All my instincts are off, and I'm becoming easily surprised and stunned. I used to have perfect reflexes and instincts. That's not the case anymore.

Whoever the man, my saviour, is, he has what appears to be dark brown hair, that could just be because of the dark, and a lithe frame. He looks familiar but I can't figure out how I know him.

Dragging my eyes away from him, I stare

towards the creature, only there isn't one of them. There are at least five of those damn creatures heading towards us. The person besides me pulls out his own weapon, a broad sword and prepares for battle. A broad sword for such a lithe person isn't common. Something in the back of my mind is blaring a siren, but for what, I'm not sure.

Still, I follow his lead. With the mace in one hand and my multi tool in the other, I'm ready. Or at least as ready as I'll ever be.

When the creatures come towards us, I swipe out with the mace, connecting with its skull in a jarring thud. The creature bellows, but not in pain, in fury. Can these creatures even feel pain? Every hit I've made to them hasn't resulted in the typical response to that of pain.

With each swing of the weapon, I find myself moving as though in a dance. With each hit, my blood hums in my veins and my senses come alive. My instincts finally start picking back up and the more my mind focuses on the battle, the less scattered my mind is.

The blood in the air calls to me. The rage from the creatures fuels my own. Their bellows call to the predator inside me. And like any good predator, I attack my prey.

Just as I'm getting into the swing of things, with two of the creatures dead on the ground. I'm tackled. Again!

"Fucking piece of shit," I holler out.

Teeth sink into my gut. I scream. Pain burns through me attempting to freeze me up. But I use the pain to fuel me. The multi-tool goes to his neck, and I heave through the creature's flesh. My attack doesn't kill the creature, but certainly distracts the damn thing.

It removes its teeth from me, bellowing in fury and the mystery man takes the creatures head off. He pants, clearly as out of breath as I am after the attack. Offering me his hand, he pulls me off the ground and we both analyse the bodies littering the ground.

"Are you alright?" he asks me.

Well, isn't that a loaded question. Am I alright? My stomach is torn up bad enough that I worry I'll need to go to hospital. Then again, I'm pretty sure supernaturals can heal from most things, and truthfully, I have no idea how I'd explain my injuries to a doctor, especially if the doctor was human. 'Hey doc, I got attacked by a cannibalistic monster, but don't worry, I'll likely heal in a couple of days,' that probably wouldn't go over well. A padded room would likely be my home for the next few years, if not my entire life.

"Sure. Thank you for your help," I say, instead of trying to overcomplicate matters. "Do you have a name?"

"My pleasure, and of course I do, Freyja," he offers with a soft smile. "But that will come later. I'll be seeing you soon," he adds, and before my eyes he just disappears.

Poof! He's gone. I'm left in the middle of the street, with bodies littering the ground. I should call someone about it, but exhaustion weighs at me and I really don't want to have to deal with all the questions. So, I don't. I pick up my belongings, including the mace the man gave me, and head away from the crime scene, wincing as the wounds on my body pull and throb. I'll have to deal with them as soon as I can.

It's only after I've started walking home, that I realise something startling. He knows my name. He knew me. So, I was right in my thought that he looks familiar. But where the hell do I know him from.

Close to home, my legs try to give out. Every inch of my body burns and aches. All I want to do is fall into bed and sleep for a week, but I have work tomorrow.

Once at home, I head to the bathroom and strip off. Staring in the mirror, I grimace at the angry lines and teeth marks spreading across my ribs and stomach. The torn flesh throbs and bleeds. Again, I consider a hospital, but I quickly brush that thought off. I will not go there and have to attempt to explain what went on. All the supernatural have, are the healers, and if I go to the estate in this state, then my friends will kick up a fuss and never leave me alone. I know they will, despite only knowing them a few days. Also, they would ask even more questions than the humans would, and I really can't be dealing with that shit.

I collect the first aid kit from the cabinet beneath the sink, and start cleaning all the injuries. Once they've all been bandaged up, I fall into bed and sink into sleep.

CHAPTER 13

Groaning, I grapple for my phone on the bedside table, only it isn't there. Blinking away the sleep, I slowly sit myself up, hoping the newfound dizziness will pass. Every part of my body hurts, and my stomach is screaming in pain. When the dizziness doesn't abate, I attempt to get out of bed. As my feet touch the ground, I stand myself up and my legs give out. I crumple to the floor, gasping at the worsening pain that rips through my stomach. Nausea fills me, and I crawl as quickly as I can to the bathroom, hoping I don't throw up on the carpet.

Once in the bathroom, I lift the toilet seat up and allow the sickness to release. Despite the heaving, nothing comes out. Even though nothing leaves me, I still shake and sweat profusely, as my stomach continues to cramp trying to eject everything out. But with nothing in it, I just heave uselessly.

I'm expected at work today, but I'm tempted to call in sick. The only problem with that is that if I'm not there, Sue will probably tell Mark, and Mark will undoubtedly tell Jillian. Then Jillian will be round here being a mother hen.

Working in the food industry means that any sickness bugs are a big hazard. However, I know for a fact I don't have a sickness bug. This entire thing is all because of last night. I'm even more sure of that fact because I've never caught a sickness bug, not once in my entire life. Hell, I've never even had the flu.

So, instead of wallowing in pain and misery, I pull myself together. Dragging myself up from the toilet, I splash cold water in my face. Putting on the first clean clothes I pull from my wardrobe, I put them on, before making my way downstairs. Flicking on the kettle, I draw up the energy to make a cup of tea. After three cups of tea, I have a little more energy than I did before.

Before I leave, I pull out my first aid kit again, and check on my wounds. Pulling the dressing off, I gag at the sight of my stomach. It's a mess. Although, it's thankfully stopped bleeding. Even so it's not exactly good when black goo seems to be seeping from the torn-up flesh, and despite it not bleeding, it is still very open. I clean the injury thoroughly with sterile alcohol wipes and wrap a fresh bandage around it to help keep it clean.

With my wound sorted, I head out and to the bakery. The walk is far more tiring than it usually is, but as I spot the bakery, I pull in as much of the exhaustion and pain as I can, and plaster on an expression I hope will portray that everything is perfectly fine.

Opening the door to Sue's Sanguine Sweets, the bell chimes and I wince at the noise, as it stabs into my eardrums. Christ, I wish painkillers worked on me. Despite me never getting sick with common illnesses, it doesn't mean I've never injured myself. We learnt very quickly that most painkillers don't have any impact on me, and only an extremely large dose of very strong ones have any affect. I suspect that was all part of my supernatural heritage.

"Morning Freyja," Sue sings. She looks as radiant as ever with her brown and white hair piled into a messy bun, and a gorgeous blue maxi dress swaying as she moves. She looks to me, and her eyes go wide. "Are you alright? You're looking rather pale."

"I'm fine," I say attempting a smile. "Just

hungover," I add, hoping that will appease her. She chuckles. Score. Now to get through the rest of the day.

At lunch, I've just about had enough of this day. I'm counting down the hours until I finish. Why do I feel worse today than I did when I was attacked in the cemetery? Surely that should have left a worse feeling, than a little bite and scratch.

Usually when I get injured, it starts to feel better only hours after it happened. This doesn't seem to be getting any better, only worse. I'm starting to wonder if I'll have to go see the healers at the estate.

"Morning Jailbird," King Xander chirps, coming into the bakery. When his eyes land on me, he has the same expression as just about everyone has all day. Do I really look that bad? "I can understand why Sue called me. What happened? Are you feeling alright?"

"Why the fuck would Sue call you?" I curse.

"Because she knows I care. Now answer the question."

The damn man needs to learn to keep his concern to himself. He doesn't know me. It doesn't matter if I want to jump him every time I see him. That still doesn't mean I need his help.

"I'm fine. Hungover is all," I offer.

"Nice try. Jill told me you can handle your alcohol, and that you haven't drunk in a few years," he smiles. I wince, knowing exactly the last time I drunk and the reason I stopped. Or at least that was the last time I drunk to excess. I'm not surprised I was convinced I had drunk earlier on in the week, when I was attacked in the cemetery, but it's true I don't really drink anymore.

Fucking Jill and her fucking mouth. "I was attacked on my way home last night. But I'm fine," I offer, attempting to appease the beast.

"Well, I'll be the judge of that," he says seriously. "You're going to the healers to be checked out."

I attempt to fight him on his choice. Jack had always called me stubborn. Always claimed I had to fight him on every decision he ever made. He never caught on to the fact he made stupid decisions, hence why I always fought him.

Still, I look at Xander and shake my head. I don't need to go to the healers. I don't need to be poked and prodded by strangers, just for them to tell me I'll get better in time.

Unfortunately, by shaking my head my vision swims. Xander rushes to my side and steadies me, but my vision keeps swimming.

Closing my eyes in an attempt to shake off my unsteadiness, doesn't help. Weakness seems to fill every inch of my body. My legs give out and Xander clings to me.

When the weakness doesn't get any better, Xander scoops me into his arms, and I can't help but rest my head on his chest. Taking a deep breath, I'm filled with his intoxicating scent. It's all masculine and it's all him. Exhaustion seems to settle in, as a feeling of safety and security envelops me.

I'm asleep before he's even carried me out the bakery.

I'm awoken when Xander stops the car. Blinking my eyes doesn't help clear the fuzziness, but I can still tell we are at the estate. I attempt to open the car door and stand, but just like before, my body doesn't want to cooperate. Xander rushes to my side and scoops me into his arms before I can face plant the floor. Jack may have been right about me being a bit stubborn. Again, Xander's masculine scent swamps me and I find the aches and pains ease, as my body relaxes, and my sight slightly clears. Why does he bring on this sort of reaction? I'll have to speak to Jill and the girls to get some information. Although they do love to gossip, so it might not be the best idea. I'd never hear the end of it.

He carries me through the double door entrance.

"Someone get the healers," he calls out, and chaos ensues as people part to make way for us, and one of the guards run to fetch the healers.

We make it to the healing room in record time. I look around spotting numerous beds lining the walls, with partitions jotted about to allow privacy. Various equipment also lines the walls in a haphazard style that gives ease of access to it. It's the sort of system where things are simply pushed out of the way and left there. But judging by the almost brand-new state of nearly all the equipment, it doesn't get used often. Likely because supernaturals heal quicker than humans.

The healers greet Xander and encourage him to lay me down on the bed. Almost instantly, I want to sleep again. I'm just so tired.

"Freyja, I need you to open your eyes for me," one of the healers orders, and it's an effort to obey. But still, I manage to. The healer is a pretty brunette with pale blue eyes. Her porcelain, flawless skin, makes me think she's a vampire like Alexis. In fact, the more I look, the more she seems to hold a lot of similarities to my vampire friend.

"Can you tell me what happened?" she asks.

"She said she was attacked last night," Xander fills in.

"Attacked by who? Were you injured?" she asks me.

"Cemetery creature," I offer, not remembering the name of it.

I attempt to pull my shirt up, but I can't draw enough strength to do so. All day I've managed to keep going, but suddenly my entire body feels like it's shutting down. It's as though all the life has been drained from me, and it's a fight to keep myself awake. Moving is out of the question.

"Do I have permission to cut your top off?" the healer asks me, when she spots what I'm trying to do. Nodding my consent, she quickly brandishes a pair of scissors that make quick work in turning my shirt to scraps.

Xander's and the healer's eyes narrow in on the injuries, as the healer peels back the dressings I had put on them. I cry out in pain. The pair cringe when they see the state of my stomach. Maybe I should have come here yesterday. It's never a good sign when a medical professional, which the healers are, cringe at your injuries.

"Wasn't it a wraith that attacked in the cemetery?" the healer asks. The confusion evident in her voice.

"Supposedly. None of this makes sense though, because if she was truly attacked by a wraith, she'd be dead. We all know that," Xander offers.

Despite his claim that 'we' all know that. I don't know that. I mean, I may have been told at some point, but I honestly don't really pay all that much attention, unless it's reading peoples intentions in body language. In which case, I'm very observant and focused. People bore me, and the monotony of what most like to talk about, doesn't interest me. I've found you can just nod your head and say 'yeah' or 'hum' a few times and they're none the wiser.

Although that can sometimes be a bad idea. Once someone was talking to me about how sad it was that someone's pet had died. Since I wasn't paying them any attention, I had a faux smile plastered on my face as I nodded my head and said 'yeah'. I seemed like such a heartless bitch, and if it wasn't for Jill, I wouldn't have even known what I had done.

"It couldn't have been then," the healer states, pulling me back to hers and Xander's conversation. "Maybe it's just a look alike. I'll take bloods and run tests to figure out the toxin currently in her system. For the time being she needs her rest," the healer explains to Xander, and he nods.

He goes to leave the room, and I pry my eyes open. Where's he going? Why's he leaving me? As the healer starts placing little sticker things on my chest, a machine blares its dire warnings. Xander comes back instantly, looking panicked. Almost instantly my heart rate slows back down to a normal pace.

"I think you should stay your highness. Just until she's asleep," the healer exclaims.

A needle pierces my hand and I attempt to jerk away. Xander holds me down, as the healer sticks a large plaster in place around it, to keep it in. An IV catheter. The healer draws my blood. Five vials of the stuff, then proceeds to connect me to some fluids. All the while Xander holds me down. I don't want to be in here. I want to be in my own bed, asleep.

As the healer walks off to do something else, Xander asks, "How many of these supposed wraiths attacked you?"

"Five," I offer, just as the healer comes back with a needle in her hand.

This time, I manage to nearly roll off the bed, before Xander stops me. I'm apparently stubborn to the very end.

"Don't worry my dear. This is just something to help you sleep," the healer says, and I still jerk and attempt to escape. What little energy I had, is quickly drained away by my exertion, making my systems weak to the powerful drugs the healer pushes through my IV.

Within seconds my sight goes even fuzzier. Within a minute I'm away in dream land, oblivious to the world around me.

CHAPTER 14

Soft silk cocoons my body in warmth. I never want to leave my bed. In fact, when did it get so comfortable. Turning over, I snuggle deeper into the blankets, only for a jarring pain to wake me up fully. Opening my eyes, I'm surprised to find a canopy over the bed I'm laid in. It looks really fancy, trussed up in sheer fabrics in blues and blacks. It's pretty but seems more masculine. Truthfully, it's just my style. Sitting up, I wince at the pain in my side.

My eyes take in the room, and I realise the reason for such a comfortable sleep. This isn't my bed. It's a queen-sized plush bed, with soft silk sheets in a pale blue. My guess is the mattress I'm laid on, is the most expensive thing I've ever touched, never mind slept in. Alright realistically, the canopy itself made me realise it wasn't my room, but I could have just forgotten I'd got something so luxurious.

The last thing I remember before my nap, was being at work. As my memories surface and I realise I was taken to the estate by Xander, I let out a shaky breath. At least I'm still alive. Considering the last time I was conscious, I felt like death warmed over, I'm pleasantly surprised by my recovery. Energy fills me, and no longer do I want to throw up and pass out. This doesn't seem like the sort of thing that would happen if I was dying.

If my memory is right, Xander and the medic said something about wraiths being capable of killing a supernatural. Something about their toxin being dangerous to us. Clearly that's not the case if I wasn't killed by it.

Another thought strikes me. What if it is a killer for supernaturals? Why didn't it kill me? What am I that a deadly creature didn't end my life? How did I survive at the cemetery?

Did I actually die and I'm now in heaven? This bed seems like heaven to me. But I expected to end up in hell. I was hoping to rule the place. If I'm truly dead, maybe I can ask the devil to teach me his wicked ways, and I can spend an eternity creating new punishments for wicked souls. I've always thought playing 'it's a small world' on repeat would be a very simple, but affective, torture method. Certainly, less effort than the fiery pits of hell, and likely more effective than fire torture. After all, some people like that.

With no answers to all my burning questions, and one person I know, who could possibly answer them, I pull myself from the comforting confines of the bed. I wonder if I could steal the bed. Would anyone notice me relocating it? Probably. That's a shame.

With the duvet no longer covering my body, I look down, noticing a large dressing on my stomach. That would be the reason for the pain. I carefully peel it back, only to find a small looking wound, that seems to be just about healed. It's likely that the surface has healed before the inside. Still, I'm surprised how quickly the injury has mended.

Looking around the room, I search for something to wear. Apparently, I was sleeping in the bed in my underwear. I vaguely remember something about my top, but I'm not going to fret. Injuries often mean clothing removal. Despite only being with the supernaturals a short time, I don't get the impression they'd do anything untoward, especially since the King was watching over me, and I know deep in my gut that he wouldn't do anything to harm me.

Searching the room, I find a door that leads to a walk-in wardrobe. It's filled with clothing for both males and females. Is this a spare room? Do they just keep guest rooms filled with clothing? Whatever. Then again this seems pretty extravagant for a guest bedroom. If it's not a guest bedroom, then whose room is it?

I select the first item on the rack, which happens to be a pale blue dress. I can't say I'm one for dressing up, but even I can admit how gorgeous the item is. After pulling it on, I make my way from the room not even bothering to find any shoes.

People give me odd looks as I walk down the stairs. I stare back. What is everyone's problem?

"Where is Xander?" I ask a random person, on my trip down the stairs.

She looks at me in surprise.

"The King is likely in his office," she explains. I look at her. "His office is on this floor right at the end of the hallway," she adds.

After thanking her, I make my way to the bottom of the flight of stairs and head in the direction she told me.

It occurs to me I should probably get used to referring to Xander as the king, but something about it doesn't sit right. He's never questioned my use of his name, so I've never considered it a problem. But I suppose if it was any other royalty, they'd have a title people were expected to use. Still, I've never been one to follow the rules, so until he mentions it, I'll just call him Xander. After he mentions it, I'll likely just come up with a different title to use on him. Probably along the lines of Dickhead or Jackass. I'm creative like that.

When I make it to the large doors, that seem to lead to his office, I'm stopped.

"Miss you can't go in there," a young woman states seriously. She's wearing a pencil skirt and a button up shirt. In her hands is a tablet, that seems to be showing a calendar app.

"Why? I need to speak to Xander," I explain.

"His highness," she emphasises, "is in a meeting."

Ignoring her, I press my ear to the door, listening in to what is being said. I've no idea where this behaviour has come from. I'm never this rude. Then again, I've never felt this attached to someone before. I should probably be concerned about that, but I can't find it in me to be.

"Miss, you need to leave," she adds urgently.

Thankfully, she doesn't try to touch me and pull me away. I've got enough instant reactions, that she'd likely end up rather injured if she was to do that.

"Fuck off would you. I'm trying to listen," I snap. Instantly, I regret my outburst because that's not like me. Even so, I can't find it in me to apologise. What the hell is wrong with me? Don't get me wrong, I snap all the time, but it's usually over a valid reason. It isn't usually because I'm doing something wrong and being asked to leave.

"I'm getting security," she states, and stomps off to fetch the guards.

With silence once again achieved, I press my ear to the door. Despite the thickness of the door, I can hear what is being said.

"The infirmary confirmed it. I don't understand how she survived. No supernaturals have ever survived, other than those like you," Xander's voice rings out. Instantly, I know he's on about the incident with me.

"I've not heard of any more of us being out there," a woman's voice states. It seems familiar, but it can't be who I think it is.

"It's possible, but usually we get a sign that there's another," a male voice adds and again it seems familiar. "Maybe because she's still transitioning, she's got her human metabolism still. Maybe that itself is what helped her survive."

Another male in the room laughs a belly laugh. "Please. Situations like this are never simple. It's possible there's another like us. But it's more likely it's something else. There's a specific number of us in existence at any one time, and although there are currently three missing from the list, I highly doubt this woman fits the profile for any of them," this male states. Thankfully I don't recognise his voice.

"Which ones are missing?" Xander asks.

"Wraith, angel of death and Jinx," the man offers.

"Well, I wouldn't say that she doesn't fit the profile of any of them. She's a violent machine," Xander offers.

"She couldn't be more violent than our daughter," the woman snorts out a laugh. "She is truly a recipe for mass destruction."

What the hell are they talking about? Can they actually follow this conversation? Who's violent? I'll kill anyone more violent than me because they're likely a bad person.

"I don't know what is going on, which is why I contacted you. She's been out for three days, and I'm concerned. Her wound has mostly healed, but she isn't waking up," Xander says. He seems distraught by this.

Maybe they aren't speaking about me. I don't think I've been unconscious that long. But if it is me, is it possible, he's just as attached to me as I am him. He seems genuinely concerned about whoever it is, and I'm going to go out on a limb and say that's not a common occurrence, since he has many people in his territory so he can't be emotionally attached to everyone. Then again, if it is me they're discussing, is it possible he's as attached to me as I am to him?

I remember the feeling of safety and security he gave me when I was injured. He didn't leave me because he knew his presence soothed me. That's not what someone who doesn't care would do. My heart flutters in my chest at the thought of him caring about me, as much as I do him. But then I have to remember he's possibly not talking about me. If it's not me, I'll destroy whoever it is. Xander is mine.

I momentarily pause. My own mind has me surprised. It almost sounds like I'm jealous, and I've never felt that before. It's so catty, and I've managed to shock myself. Shaking it off, I turn my attention back to what is being said in the closed office.

"Look, the likelihood is she won't wake up. Wraith injuries aren't simple. For some it kills quickly, for others it's a long-drawn-out situation," the woman states simply. Then adds, "as for the possibility of another like us. It isn't likely. Most are from supernatural lines. Smith isn't a supernatural line," she explains, and I go cold. So, they are on about me.

"That's her married name I believe. Not her family name," Xander offers.

Silence descends in the room. Clearly, they're all in deep thought.

"What supernatural is she?" the unfamiliar male voice asks.

"We don't know. Certainly not a standard one. She's not really shown signs of being anything. Other than heightened senses and the fact she survived, what would have been a death sentence for a human, she could be human," Xander states.

"So, she hasn't been turned. Clearly born," the familiar male states.

"Yes. She moved into your old family home. Maybe there's something there that could answer the questions," Xander offers.

My blood turns to ice. There's no way. The man and woman in there sound familiar, but it's not possible they're who I think they are. Although now that thought is in my head, I can't help but feel that is the case. With every word they say, the more I hear who I shouldn't have ever been able to hear again. I'm honestly shocked it took me so long to make the connection.

I push the door open with extreme force, and the heavy doors swing open and crash into the wall. I stare at those in the room. Xander sits on one sofa with an unknown man. His desk sat at the far end of the room, sits unused. Clearly, this is a more informal meeting.

On the opposite side of Xander, on another sofa sits two people I never thought I'd see again. The deep brown hair and pale blue eyes of the man, bears a striking resemblance to what I see in the mirror. The lighter brown hair and green eyes belong to a woman, I am so very similar in personality to.

They're dead. They had a funeral, I didn't attend. They faked it. They must have.

"You bastards," I shout. Glaring at the pair. The rage, I'm sure burns in my eyes, pierces them. Their eyes go wide, but it's Xander who speaks up first.

Seems things are about to get a whole lot more complicated.

CHAPTER 15

Xander is the one who stands up. For the first time since I met him, he looks truly murderous. It's a hot look on him and only makes me want to jump him more. I can understand why he's so angry. After all, I've just barged into his office like I own the place and called his guests bastards. He doesn't realise I have a valid reason for my anger.

"Freyja, this is Judgement and Balance. You will treat them with respect," Xander says, indicating the woman and then the man. Well that certainly sounds accurate for the pair.

"What sort of names are they, huh?" I demand of the pair. "Or is it just something else you lied to me about?"

Ignoring my outburst, Xander's shouts, "Either calm down, or I will have security get you out of this room."

I so want to reply, 'I'd love to see them try,' but I don't. Biting my tongue to stop the remark, I glare at the pair. My anger rises.

"I don't know. I want to watch the fireworks," the unknown dark skinned man states. My glare turns to him. His smirk sends me over the edge, and I surprise myself by flying for him. I literally dive bomb him. I've never done such a move before.

I land a solid punch to his jaw, and his eyes round. He flings me off him, and I go soaring through the air before crashing into the wall with a thud and a crack. Thankfully, the crack was from the wall and not my body. Climbing to my feet, I shake off the impact. It doesn't stop me, and I go for the handsome idiot again. Kicking out, I hit his ribs and he too goes flying, soaring into the air before landing harshly on Xander's desk.

"Freyja," Xander shouts. "Stop."

The unknown man swings at me and I duck, sending a rapid strike to his gut. We go back and forth hitting each other for a while. Eventually, I have him pinned and throw punch after punch into his face, attempting to wipe that fucking smile off his face. If anything, that only makes him happier. Is it possible I'm related to him, that's my sort of reaction to violence.

I stop. Straddling him, I look into his eyes. "Next time mind your own fucking business or I'll kill you," I warn him. He stays silent, looking at me with awe. Someone would have thought I'd just given him a present, rather than beating the living shit out of him. He's either some supernatural with severe issues, or he's a masochist. My money's on masochist.

Standing up, I turn to the couple. "As for you. You're dead to me. That's how you wanted it right," I state.

"My dear we never wanted that, but it was necessary," the woman says.

"Will someone explain what the hell is going on?" Xander asks. When I turn to him, he flinches back. Instead of turning away, he stares in awe at my eyes. "They're silver!"

It would seem he's finally figured out that something more is going on. Although, I have no idea what he's on about, saying my eyes are silver. They've never been silver.

"Yes. It would seem you were right; she is one of us. As for the first question. This is our daughter, Freyja Eliza Heathen," my mother states.

"Am I really your daughter? After all you faked your own death. Surely that means you don't give a flying fuck about me anymore," I state.

"She's your daughter...," Xander repeats slowly. He turns to look at the man I just beat up. He's pulled himself off the ground and is looking at me with adoration.

Anger is raging through me and I'm unable to think reasonably. As is common with me my default setting is anger and rage. No part of me is thinking calmly right now. So, I'm not exactly polite when I spit, "and who the fuck are you?"

"Lucifer," the man offers holding out his arms and moving closer to me. When he attempts to hug me, I knee him in the groin. Keeling over, he groans out, "It's a pleasure to meet you."

"Don't think I won't destroy you if you piss me off again. You may have a devilish name, but that doesn't scare me."

"What about if I was the devil? Would that scare you?" He asks. That sly grin still plastered to his face.

"Nope. I'm sure I'll be ruling that shit hole before long," I offer.

"Well, I can teach you the 'how' if you want. I'd love for you to visit me. After all, you've got plenty of cousins there," he explains.

My brain promptly fizzles out. Cousins? Where?

"What are you talking about?" I ask.

"My dear," my father starts, "this is Lucifer. The Devil, as he is commonly known. He lives in hell. He has seven daughters named after the seven deadly sins. No this isn't a joke."

He's the actual devil. Holy shit? All that bullshit's real?

"Wait, does that mean that dickhead is real?" I ask, pointing upwards to indicate he who gets called God. I've always thought that was rather stuck up. There are plenty of Gods and Goddesses believed to exist. What earns him the name of God? Everyone else has an actual name. It's rather stuck up of him.

"Yep. He's your... go with uncle to avoid confusion," Lucifer states.

Holy fucking shit. To think my parents weren't going to tell me any of this. Instead, they faked their fucking deaths and left me alone in the world.

"Holy fucking shit," Xander swears, glancing between my mother, father, Lucifer and me. "My mate is the family of the fucking devil." He lets out a laugh. I think this is all a bit too much for him.

Ignoring his shock, I too look between them all. What on earth is going on? Since when have I got cousins and an uncle. Wait, if Lucifer is my uncle, does that mean my mother or father is a brother or sister to him? Or is it similar to the 'God' situation and it's just easier for me to call him uncle, then to add on all the greats to that shit show.

If I come from a family of such notorious supernaturals, why was I kicked out for not showing a supernatural side. Surely, they would have known I was supernatural if the majority of my genetics come from other supernaturals.

"Hey now," Lucifer starts, addressing Xanders comments, "don't let her grandmother hear you say that. She might just take it as you not wanting to be part of the family." The grin on his face makes me think that would be a violent encounter if that was the case. Although I have no idea why they're talking about Xander being part of the family. Alright, I have the hots for him, but that doesn't mean we're going to get married and have babies.

"Wait, Papi and Gigi are alive?" I ask, when it finally occurs to me what the devil had said. Surely that is who he's referring to. I'm sure I don't have other grandparents, then again, I didn't know the devil was my fucking uncle either.

With a guilty look, mum replies, "Yeah. I

probably should have told you as soon as you knew we were alive."

"You think," I mutter.

Dad remains quite and looks solemn as though his own mind is driving him to despair. Lucifer on the other hand has a huge grin on his face and is watching the exchange between me and mum with rapt fascination. Likely expecting us to break out in a fight. Considering she's judgement, and I'm violent as hell, it's likely expected.

But for the first time in my life, I don't fight. Instead, I take a deep steadying breath and focus on calming my frayed nerves. I impress myself when it actually works.

"Alright," I start, sighing out any remaining frustration, "mum and dad are alive. Gigi and Papi are alive. The devil is my uncle, and everything is slightly fucked up," I add to myself. The others can obviously hear me, but they keep their mouths shut.

Deciding to switch topics, I ask, "What is with all these attacks? Didn't you call them wraiths?" I ask Xander, but also speak to everyone in the room.

"Yes, we confirmed they are definitely wraiths," my dad offers. "Typically, that's a death sentence for supernaturals, but when it didn't kill you, and the results of the blood tests were indicative of a wraith, King Alexander contacted the immortal truths council to give some advice," he adds. I've always loved how he talks. Always sophisticated and soft. Now that I know more about him, he's likely a lot older than he looks and carries his behaviours from an older time.

"So why didn't I die?" I ask. It seems like a logical question.

"Because you're like us," Lucifer offers, as though that explains everything. I glare at him. Rolling his eyes he adds, "You're part of the Heathen clan. Ten percent of us are immortal truths, the others are often immortals that can very rarely be killed, compared to supernaturals in general. Obviously supernaturals have extremely extended lives and could be considered immortal, but there are more things that can kill them compared to immortals, hence the distinction," Lucifer explains. Not wanting to admit that still doesn't make all that much sense, I move on from the conversation.

"So, what do we do about the wraiths?" I ask.

"Our supernatural guard forces are trained in the removal of wraiths, despite them not being a common occurrence. I've issued patrols of the town for all hours of the day, and Balance and Judgment have offered their assistance in training the supernatural guards in skills that only they know," Xander offers, and I admit that sounds like a good plan.

Although part of me wonders why they're attacking in the first place. What is their end game? Everybody knows attacks always have an end goal, so what is there's. Figuring they know better than me, I let it go. I highly doubt they'd want a newbie supernatural to be interfering. After all, they're the ones with the experience. My only experience comes from beating the shit out of dickheads.

"You need to start training as well," my mum orders, and I roll my eyes. She and all my family had all played a role in teaching me self-defence as a child, and when I was older, they would teach me more advanced skills. I've continued that training throughout my time away. That being said, I'm certainly not going to argue with her, since it allows me to work out any frustration, as well as keeping me fighting fit.

"When are you posting the patrols?" I ask, wondering if I'll end up being put on the patrol after they've assessed my skills.

"We started it three days ago, after I bought you back to the estate," Xander offers, and the lost look that crosses his face has me thinking the possibility of my death affected him more than I expected.

Gaping, I screech "I've been unconscious for three days!" How could I have been unconscious for so long? I've got shit to do, people to beat up, cakes to bake. Shit, the bakery.

Nodding his head, he explains, "that's part of the reason I contacted the Immortals council. I was concerned, and when I spoke to my dad for advice, he told me to trust them. I didn't understand why, but now all has become clear."

"Can your father see into the future or something?" I ask Xander.

"No, but he did receive information from a seer about the coming events. Nothing too specific, but it was incredibly important that we trust these... dickheads," he offers, with a sly grin to me. A smile stretches my face as I realise the respect he had for them before, has been replaced by disgust at their treatment of their daughter.

If I didn't love this guy before, I certainly do now.

Holy shit. I love him.

I barely know him. But I love him...

CHAPTER 16

At work the following day, I'm upbeat for the first time in a long time.

Xander had tried to get me to rest for another couple of days, fretting that I wasn't ready to go back to work. Unfortunately for him, I'm not the sort of person who can sit back and do nothing. Also unfortunate for him, there were three immortals there who all confirmed that I was in fact fit as a fiddle, and perfectly fine to go back to work.

So today, I'm back, and Sue is pleased to see me.

"Of course, I worried about you. Supernaturals don't get sick often and when we do it's severe," she explains. Despite only knowing her for a short time, she cares so much and so quickly. Although I get the impression that's only

157

for people who have earnt her kindness. Just like all supernaturals, she has this predatory grace to her.

We get to work baking the goods, and because I've finally accepted supernaturals are real, she even tells me the secret to the other range of baked goods we offer.

"It's a blood substitute," she explains, and I gawk. Laughing, she explains, "It has the taste and nutrition of blood. Food with this substitute in is easier for blood drinking supernaturals to consume. It's not actual blood however, that's reserved for their proper meals."

Holy shit. That's so clever. Once I'd have considered that to be disgusting and freaky as hell, but now that's not the case. Despite everything still being rather overwhelming, I've mostly come to terms with it all. Something else occurs to me. I've eaten some of those pastries and a deep overwhelming hunger had filled me. For some reason since that day, it hasn't returned. Why haven't I felt that hunger?

Sue's expression turns to one of curiosity. "You've eaten some of them. Haven't you?" Nodding my head, her expression turns to understanding, "And what did you think?"

"Best thing I've ever eaten," I answer honestly. "Although it did create a deep hunger."

"How's that hunger now?" she asks.

"Alright. I slept off the hunger and haven't really been that bothered since. Now that I think about it, I haven't really been that bothered about eating at all," I explain, frowning.

She bites the inside of her cheek while contemplating something. "So, you're not dependant on a particular substance for survival, which rules out most supernatural," she mumbles out loud. Not exactly talking to me, but more working through her theory out loud.

She rushes off into the other kitchen while I continue baking some of the goods for opening. About five minutes later, she comes back in with a mug in her hand.

"Drink up," she orders.

Taking the mug, I peer into it gaping at the deep crimson in the cup. Giving it a sniff, a metallic scent hits me. I expect disgust to hit me, but it doesn't. Instead that hunger from before comes back, and my stomach grumbles. Holy shit, she's just given me a mug of blood, and I'm wanting to drink it.

Not daring to think too long on it all. I salute her with the mug, before putting it to my lips. As the blood hits my tongue, flavour bursts, and I can't stop the groan that escapes. It's fucking gorgeous. I know for a fact it shouldn't taste like this, but I'm not sure if this is because I'm a supernatural of some kind, or whether she added something to it. I guzzle the rest down, loving the taste and loving how it fills a hole in my stomach I didn't realise was there.

"Well certainly a blood drinker of some sort," Sue offers, adding a smile at my shocked expression. "Not a vampire as you would only be able to consume blood, with the exception of the Sanguine range. Something that consumes both blood and food," she adds. All the while I get the impression, she's not so much talking to me, but is more working through all the information for her own sake.

We get back to work and Sue remains mostly quiet. The look of concentration on her face, makes me think she's still running through possibilities for the type of supernatural I am. After a while, my curiosity is peaked on a different topic. It's one I've not been able to pull from my mind, and since I didn't want to bother Xander and everyone with my relentless questions, I had pushed them to the back of my mind for the time being. Now however, that curiosity returns full force.

"Hey Sue, do you know much about wraiths?" I ask.

She looks up at me, as though startled. I

know that reaction. It's the reaction of someone so caught up in their own minds, they forgot other people exist.

"Wraiths are nasty pieces of work," she starts. "For starters, they are the result of necromancy, but they are dead supernaturals which is why they are so difficult to kill. Obviously, decapitation works in dropping them, as does a strike to the heart. However as simple as that sounds, it isn't, because they truly are superhuman. Or I suppose super supernatural would be more applicable."

"They're stronger than supernaturals?" I ask her.

Despite engaging in conversation, we both continue working with the ease of muscle memory. I'm still surprised this has all been so easy for me to pick up, despite only doing it a short amount of time. At least at this stage it's not so much preparing batter as it is rolling pastry out, so I don't need to double check any of the recipes.

"Yes. A lot stronger," she confirms. "It's not even just their physical strength and senses that are improved either, because of the dead nature of them, and the magic used, their skin and body itself is even stronger," she explains.

Frowning, I think over my past experiences

with the creatures. I've battled with wraiths before and yes it was difficult, but the way she makes it sound, makes me think it should have been even worse than how I found it to be.

"If they are dead supernaturals, how did they come to be wraiths?" I ask.

"Typically, a group of magic wielders are responsible. Witches or mages, sometimes even warlocks," she explains. I've no idea what distinguishes warlocks from the other two categories but I'm not even going to touch that question at the moment. "Warlocks are male Mages," she adds. I swear to the devil himself; this woman can read minds. "The important thing to remember when it comes to wraiths, is that they don't act of their own freewill. They are merely puppets with a master."

"If you were to kill the master...," I trail off, allowing Sue to fill in the blank. Afterall, there are a couple of options. The wraiths could fly free, and start acting on some sort of instinct, or they could die.

"They die," she confirms.

Well, that gives me some hope this situation can be sorted out.

"So, we know it's a magic wielder responsible. That must shorten down the pool of possible attackers," I state.

"Not quite my dear. It's important to remember that despite a magic wielder being required for the spell to raise the dead. All supernaturals have some natural magic. It's what makes us supernatural after all. Anyone could be the one pulling the strings of the entire situation. It's only a magic wielder that needs to perform the spell," she explains, and my little bit of hope is dashed.

"And just because they performed the spell it doesn't mean they are necessarily a criminal, right?" I add, realising where this is going. "They could be being forced to perform the spell in some way, by the supernatural who's actually pulling the strings."

Fuck!

We lapse into silence again as we both mull this information over. It seems I'm not the only one thinking about the situation. Sue seems just as thoughtful as me. Almost as though speaking through the knowledge on wraiths has her remembering the facts, which in turn has her considering the current state of things.

"Has there been any new situations in the magical community?" I ask. Surely if the wraiths are targeting supernaturals it would be because of some event or situation. Being so new to the community, I wouldn't know exactly what is going on.

"Not really," she offers. "Usual stuff. This supernatural celebrity has done this or that. One faction or another is wanting more power. It's always the same old, same old. But most of these get resolved peacefully. When you have a ton of strong supernatural people, all with the ability to swiftly dispatch someone, you learn to use your words. Plus, the majority of all supernaturals, no matter how much they may hate one another, can always agree on one thing. Wraiths aren't something to be messed with."

"How long have the wraiths been attacking the community?" I ask.

"The first encounter I heard about was when you were attacked at the cemetery," she offers. "All the patrols that have been wandering around recently haven't found any trace of other wraiths. We assumed it was an isolated event, until you were injured by one. How did you escape it?"

It only just occurs to me that she doesn't know what happened during the attack, other than it was a wraith. Did I even tell them I was helped?

"There was five of them. Honestly, I didn't think I'd manage to fend one of them off because all I had was a multi-tool and pepper spray. But someone else showed up and brought me a mace to use. He looked familiar but I can't…," I trail off as an image of my grandad pops into my mind.

As a child I was shown pictures of my grandparents as well as my parents when they were younger. The one of my Papi always stuck in my mind because in a weird way it always reminded me of me. I was always called my Papi's little double because despite being different genders, I was basically a female version of him.

"Papi," I say out loud. But saying it out loud has me shaking my head. No, not Papi. Someone who is similar in build and look to him but also someone who knows my weapon of choice. "It's someone similar to Papi but not Papi. I know in my gut it wasn't him, but I'm not entirely sure who it was," I explain to Sue, who had been watching me quizzically.

"You were attacked by five wraiths and lived to tell the tale. Fucking hell. Well, whoever it was who helped you, deserves some praise. There's no way you would've survived without him," she states. Then she gives me a once over and adds, "Then again, maybe you would have."

Not for the first time I look at her with just as much curiosity. "What are you?" I ask her.

She smiles softly, "I'm a siren seer. I'm a very rare supernatural, hence why people often come to me for advice, including the king. I've been around a very long time, and I've seen civilisations rise and fall. I can't read minds, but I can read people. I also see future potentials," she explains.

"Future potentials?" I question.

"Nobody's future is set in concrete. The choices made; influence the path you take. It's the reason I don't share my visions with others," she explains. It makes sense. So many times, I've watched movies with future sight in them, and I've thought, you shouldn't be sharing that information because it influences a person's actions. Ultimately nothing is fixed and there are many potentials for everyone. "I do often give insight and wise words to help people along the path I believe to be the most beneficial for the individual, but it allows them to make their own decisions," she adds.

She uses her powers to help people, without going over the top and having people alter the way they behave just so they don't encounter a particular outcome. That's smart.

"Any wise words for me oh great one," I joke.

With a sinister grin, she says, "Bite him. Bite him hard!"

CHAPTER 17

The following day, I head over to the estate. I'd been asked to attend training today, which I'm excited about. It's been some time since I last had a proper training session and I'm looking forward to finding out how training with supernaturals will differ from training with humans. I'm assuming the violence it's kicked up a few levels since supernaturals are harder to kill. At least I'm really hoping so. I love a good bit of bloodshed in the morning.

As soon as I step inside the giant training room, adrenaline fills me, and a huge smile stretches my face. I forgot how much I love physical activity, especially when it comes with violence.

All the usual equipment, like punching bags, mats and weights, have been shunted aside.

Now everyone stands surrounding a group of supernatural. All seem eager to get on with whatever training we are doing today.

"Freyja," Alexis calls as she comes bounding over to me. "It's good to see you here. We're about to start, come on."

I follow her towards the large group of assembled people. If I understood this right, this particular training session is for Supernatural guard force only, and it's being run by my parents. It's not often a training session is led by anyone, and usually they just do their own workout and maybe spar with others. But because my parents are here, they want to teach some new skills.

Despite me hoping for some bloodshed, I'm concerned it would be me dishing out the violence. Since I'm not part of the guard force, I'm not sure how much I'll be allowed to do. But if not, I'll just have to start a fight with one of my family members to burn off the energy that always seems to course through me.

Alexis pushes her way through the crowd, and I follow in her lead, being more vicious in shoving people out of my way. Some of those we push aside get really angry, but one look at my face and they make the good choice of stepping down. I may already have a bit of a reputation.

Soon we get to the front. I pause as I stare at

the five people at the front. My mother, father and lucifer are somewhat expected. From the little I know about the devil, he's a busybody who loves sticking his nose where it doesn't belong. What is surprising is the two other people. Both look younger than when I last saw them, but now I know they are supernatural, it's easier to see that they are the same people I once knew.

Squealing in excitement, I charge at the pair. First, I hug my Gigi and squeeze the living shit out of her, which she quickly reciprocates. I then follow it by beating on my Papi like I used to. After we've both gotten some hits in, I give him a massive squeeze as well. I was obviously angry at my parents, but I don't feel the same anger towards my grandparents, which is odd, but then again despite loving my grandparents and parents equally, I had a better connection with my grandparents, especially with my Papi. It's also slightly less jarring to see them since I already know my parents faked their deaths, so in some way I must have subconsciously been expecting it.

"Holy shit, she just hugged Mother Nature and Karma," I hear people whispering throughout the room.

Releasing my granddad, I turn towards Alexis who seems a little bit surprised but not as much as others.

"Who's Mother Nature and Karma?" I ask her.

"We are deary," Gigi replies chipperly.

"Wait, what?" I stammer out. Not able to believe all this to be true. Mother nature isn't a person, it's just how everyone refers to the environment.

"We let the humans believe we don't exist. It's more fun that way," she explains.

"And Papi is Karma," I ask. They nod their heads. "So, every time I said Karmas a bitch. I really meant Papi's a bitch?" I state.

The cackle my Grandmother gives out is music to my ears. I've missed it so much. Even my mother and father laugh and for just a short amount of time it feels like we are a family again.

"Wait, so who came first, you or the dickhead up there?" I ask Gigi. Obviously using Dickhead as my term for God.

"Me, obviously. That little shit has nothing on me, and he better remember that. If he doesn't, I'll smack his backside like when he was a child," Gigi offers, and I pause. Is she implying what I think she's implying.

"He's our son," Papi explains, and I gape. Holy fucking shit.

"Wait, if he's your son and dad is your

son as well, does that mean they're brothers?" I ask. It seems like a stupid question, but I thought my dad and lucifer were brothers. My mind is a jumble, and I can't figure out which way is up. Then again, I swear the devil made a comment about God being my uncle, so I suppose that would be the case. All three of them being siblings.

"Of course, deary," Gigi explains, and I gape.

There haven't been many occasions I've been too stunned to speak, but in this instance, I am. My dad has brothers, who are God and Lucifer. How the hell did that work? Although it's nice to finally know the answer to the question, is Lucifer Gods son or brother. Mythology can't seem to decide.

"Okay. Fine. I won't freak out about that. Anyway, please move on before I lose the plot," I state, giving my parents and grandparents a pleading look.

I'm not even going to bother trying to get Lucifer to help move this topic along, because he seems to be rather smitten with himself, and is clearly loving all the drama. Or maybe he just really liked me calling his... brother, ... a dickhead.

Thankfully, my parents move the proceedings along and get to work discussing techniques to take down wraiths. I'm even more thankful Sue had told me about wraiths yesterday or I would have felt like an idiot.

"I need a volunteer to fight Karma," My mother asks the room. I'm unsure the purpose of this but when Alexis comes forward, I realise I'm about to find out.

"Fantastic," my Papi states, giving Alexis a friendly but sinister smile. It's one that says, 'I'm nice, but I'm going to kick your ass'. He would.

"So, Karma is going to play the role of a wraith. Being an immortal truth comes with added strength, speed and senses as you all know," my mother explains to the room. When she smiles to me, I realise she's explaining it all for my sake. I'm not even embarrassed. "Alexis you are to treat Karma as though he is a wraith. Your aim is to kill him. Don't worry it won't stick." Everyone chuckles at this.

I vaguely remember Lucifer explaining this. Despite most supernaturals having extended lifespans compared to that of humans, they still have the potential to die. Then there are immortals and immortal truths. I'm not sure on the difference between the two. But I do remember Lucifer saying that immortal truths cannot die.

"There are no rules to this fight. But

remember, one swipe of the claw or a bite from a wraith will kill you. If Karma does either of those to you, you are dead and that's the end of the fight," Gigi, or Mother Nature, explains.

Alexis takes up a fighting stance and watches my Papi with serious intent. I was right, she certainly has a lethal side to her small frame and extremely friendly personality. Although certainly not enough lethality to take my Papi down. I would know, I fought him countless times. Still when Karma moves towards her, she moves swiftly with grace and practiced ease. Although, it's over quickly when Karma manages to cut her. Just like that the fight is over.

This pattern continues. A guard comes forward to battle with one of my family. They inevitably don't kill them, and instead get killed. It becomes clear that wraiths truly are incredibly difficult to kill. How the hell did I manage it?

"Freyja you're up," Papi calls me. I blink in surprise. This training session is for the guards, I'm not a guard. I honestly have no idea what I'm doing here, other than the fact I was ordered to come. Still, I don't mind fighting my Papi. Especially since, despite my happiness in seeing him again, he did in fact fake his own death.

Stepping up to the circle drawn on the floor, I face my grandfather with murderous intent.

Pulling my mace from its holster, I prepare to fight.

"She's not a guard," someone calls, sounding concerned.

It's Lucifer who replies, "Don't fret. She'll be fine. He probably won't be."

Silence descends around the room, and everyone seems to hold their breaths in anticipation of the upcoming fight. My anger boils up and adrenaline pumps through my veins. My eyes seem to focus in on my target, my hearing zeros in on any sound coming from my Papi. Every inch of me tenses and releases ready to fight.

Papi moves, only he seems to move slowly. With ease, I swipe out with my mace, nailing my grandfather in the chest and quickly spin out of the way of his swiping hand. Again, he goes to attack, and I swipe out again, smashing the mace into his cheek with an audible crack. As my adrenaline burns its way through me and my anger rises, I find myself moving automatically.

I strike and smash Karma with my mace. Blood spurts from open wounds. When he's too stunned to get up from the floor, I pounce. Without conscious thought, I sink my teeth into his neck taking a couple of gulps of blood before tearing his throat out. Despite him being down and bleeding out, I sink my mace into his skull once more for good measure. Afterall, destroying the brain, destroys a wraith.

I stand up, not even exerted. As the adrenaline and anger starts to fade slightly, I remember I have an audience. Turning around, I find the entire room stood in shocked silence. Even my family seem surprised. What did I do that was so surprising? Kill my Papi? Even they said, I can't permanently kill him.

"She's a berserker," my mother says softly. "She's like Dad."

Her words hit me, and I frown at the term. Berserker? What the hell is a berserker?

"Surely that counts as a loss," someone's voice echoes through the hall. All eyes, including my own, turn to him. "She came into contact with his blood," he states.

"Are you unaware that she's immune to wraiths? Or did you forget the kings ma…," Alexis stops herself from saying something. "Or did you forget the woman the King bought into the estate after she was attacked and poisoned?" she states.

"That was true?" he asks.

"Look at her eyes and you tell me," Alexis states.

The man does. When he looks me in the

eyes, his own seem to go extremely wide and he gulps. Backing away slowly, he mumbles an apology before hiding in the back of the group.

A gasp pulls me from the confusion. Turning, I find my Papi sitting up in a pool of his own blood. He rubs his still reforming skull with a wince.

"Great work my dear," he offers with a smile. Just like my old grandad. He'd spar with me and would always congratulate me when I landed a strike. "You're certainly growing into your supernatural side. You didn't have that strength as a child. Although I suppose that was for the best. You certainly didn't need it."

"Thanks, Papi," I state, feeling like a little girl all over again, being congratulated on a job well done.

Never in all my life did I expect that this would be my life now. Being able to kill my own grandfather and not worrying about him actually dying. Or being attacked by undead creatures in a cemetery. Or the fact I drank blood again and I liked it. Now my mother is saying I'm something called a berserker. I don't know whether I should be freaking out, or maybe even locked in a psychiatric hospital. It all seems so farfetched compared to the life I knew. But despite it all being farfetched, I can't deny I feel more like me than I ever have.

   And boy does that thought chill me!

CHAPTER 18

Heading into work the following day, I have a spring in my step and a smile plastered to my face. The shock on people's faces when I killed my Papi, plays on repeat in my mind's eye and I love it.

Part of me feels like I should be horrified that I was willing to kill my grandfather so easily. But another part of me realises the truth in what he said, he isn't so easy to permanently kill. The fact he's turned back the clock on his age is enough for me to know there is more at play here, than just standard supernatural behaviour. But added to that is the way my family is revered in the community; it tells me all I need to know.

"Morning," Sue greets me. "I heard you killed your Grandfather and scared the shit out of the Guard Force yesterday."

Her sources likely involve Jill, Alexis, Rosemary or Elana. Those girls love to gossip and come into the bakery most days. My money is on Jill or Alexis, since Jill knows everything, and Alexis was there.

"I did," I confirm.

I'm expecting to be scolded for doing such a thing. Maybe even a horrified look.

Instead, Sue grins at me and says, "Good girl. Glad to hear your well trained."

My shock is evident. Only when I'm so surprised I find myself stunned, do I force myself to consider what is normal for Supernaturals. Supernaturals are used to the brutality that comes with it. From what I know they are violent because they can withstand such violence. Unlike humans who are considerably more frail. I'm also still thinking as though I am a human and that I work with humans. To humans, me killing someone would be abhorrent and I would be arrested and thrown into prison for such a crime. Here, it's accepted, or at least accepted in certain circumstances.

I'd imagine that there are cases when murder among supernaturals is in fact a crime, but it's not as straight shooting as it is with humans. Many aspects are considered. Just last night I was researching this situation, and it went into detail about how if you start a fight, and get killed, the other person won't be punished. If you attack and kill someone for no reason, you will be punished. Any offence to a family, can be treated with deadly force, and said family is allowed to destroy the criminal party. It even includes instances where this would be allowed including kidnapping, theft of items over £1000, and murder of a family member. Although that one is conditional to the family member needing to be the one not responsible for starting the fight. Assault is also considered a valid offence to result in the vicious brutal murder of the attacker. Honestly, it's basically a society of treat people with respect or suffer the brutal consequences.

I'd gotten curious about how they know the truth of a situation, but apparently this is thanks too certain supernaturals. Seers can often see the truth of situations, and they are even more reliable if they can project their sight for others to witness. Angels and demons are also capable of discerning the truth and are usually considered reliable sources. I found it ironic that demons are considered reliable for telling the truth. But again, I believe this is where my pesky human beliefs are influencing me.

But being someone who's only recently become aware of the supernatural, it's still taking some getting used to. Especially since, unless you live in a supernatural only town, you also have to watch out for pesky human police.

"Didn't you used to work in security?" Sue asks.

"Yea," I reply.

"Why did you move to an office job then? You strike me as the sort of person who thrives in protection," she asks.

I bite my lip, debating on telling her the truth. "My partner wanted us to have a child. I was unsure. But he wanted me in a less dangerous job in order to protect his heir," I explain.

Sue grimaces. A flash of rage fills her expression before she smothers it. "He called a potential child, his heir? He made you quit a job for this purpose?" she asks, clearly wanting clarification that she'd heard me right.

I nod my head. I'd only gone along with it hoping to keep our marriage together. When we first started dating, he was a true gentleman. Kind and caring. He'd hold the door open for me and carry the shopping. He treated me like his queen. Then we got married, and he started telling me what to do. I fought it because I wasn't in the habit of taking orders. But then the guilt trips started.

"That bastard," she curses, and it's my turn

to be shocked. I've never heard her swear before and it feels kind of scandalous. Sort of like if you've got a parent who is very timid and has never sworn in their lives, suddenly comes out and swears. It's weird, but thrilling. "Why didn't you want kids?" she asks, seeming genuinely curious.

"It's not so much that I don't want them. It's more that, I'm unsure I'd have the patience to deal with them," I start to explain. "You may have noticed I'm not exactly the nicest of people, and I just worry that I won't be a good mother."

A soft smile graces her lips. "It's usually the people who worry about such a thing that turn out to be the best mothers. Don't get me wrong, raising kids is difficult, but some instinct or another kicks in and you manage."

What she says is valid. I get where she's coming from, but just because it's a possibility it doesn't stop my doubt. Although having my family back in my life, even if I am still a bit pissed off with them, would help. They all adore kids and I'm sure they'd be thrilled at the opportunity to help me out.

"Maybe," I offer Sue. "Maybe one day, later on in life. I'm out of a marriage now and don't have any prospects, so it won't be happening anytime soon."

"I wouldn't be so sure about that," she says cryptically.

My phone chimes pulling me from the conversation. I barely ever use it anymore, since the people I speak to tend to be in the town. So whoever it is, isn't someone who would just be dropping me a casual message. As soon as I see the name on the screen, I grimace.

"Speak of the devil," I mutter.

"Is everything alright?" Sue asks.

"Yea. I think so," I reply distractedly.

With my eyes still glued to the screen, I read the message. It's from my ex-husband, wanting to know where I'm staying. Apparently, he's already lost his divorce documents and is wanting a copy.

The bell on the front door rings, and I look up to see who has arrived. It must be important considering we're not even open yet. It's Xander. He has a wide smile and soft stance.

"Good morning ladies," he offers. "Sorry for coming in early. Am I alright to speak with you Sue?" he asks, to which Sue nods her head.

I don't have time to ask what Sue wants me to do first, as my phone, which is still in my hand, starts ringing. Cursing when I see the name, I answer it.

"What the fuck do you want?" I answer, not even attempting a polite greeting.

Sue and Xander look at me in question and I wave them off. Why is my ex bothering me now? It's been weeks since the divorce has been finalised and a good few months since we last saw each other.

"Nice to speak to you to. Where are you?" he asks. The stern tone tells me he's trying to pull the same bullshit he did in our marriage. Behaving as though he's the man of the house and I have to follow all his orders.

"Speak to me like that again. I dare you," I warn.

"Don't be difficult Freyja. Just tell me where you are," he orders yet again, and it makes my blood boil.

"Jack. It's none of your business where I am. If you've lost your paperwork, then speak to the lawyer, not me," I explain simply.

He lets out a disappointed sigh, as though I'm the one being an inconvenience. "This is why are marriage never worked out. You're always just so unreasonable."

"No Jack. You're the reason our marriage never worked out. You're a narcissist, who expects everyone to make way for you. To bow down at your feet. Fuck off and don't contact me again," I state, before hanging up. Why did I ever think it would be a good idea to marry the fucker? Worse, I was considering having kids with the prick.

I take a few moments to calm myself down. Every word out of my ex's mouth just seems to infuriate me. Even worse, now that I can see his true colours, I infuriate myself because I once loved the prick. I thought we'd be together for life. That we would settle down and create a life for the two of us. But obviously that was all wrong.

"Are you alright my dear?" Sue asks as she and Xander come strolling back into the room.

Pasting on a smile, I say, "Just my ex proving how much of a prick he really is." I add an eye roll to really get my point across.

"Men! Who needs 'em?" Sue states, giving a cheeky grin to Xander, who attempts to look offended.

"I'd like to point out, we aren't all arseholes," he offers.

"Have you ever married one?" Sue asks seriously.

Xander gives her a frown. "Obviously not. Although I did experiment when I was younger," he reveals.

"If you ain't ever married a bloke, you don't know what it's like," she offers.

Even I know she's just winding Xander up. Xander being who he is, eats it up and jokes around with her about it. I watch the exchange, noticing for the first time just how close he and Sue seem to be. Not in the romantic way, however. More in the parent and child sort of way. I'm almost certain Sue isn't his mother, but she seems to offer guidance and a helping hand whenever she can. But Xander is just the same. They care for one another.

In fact, the more I see Xander's interactions with everyone, the more I realise he may not be like Jack. He doesn't strike me as the sort of person to be controlling or nasty. He always strives to be friendly and welcoming, only bringing out the sterner side of him when truly necessary, and usually it's only necessary in order to protect. Like when he shouted at me to stop disrespecting three immortal truths, obviously before he realised I'm related to the jackasses. But still, in a way he was trying to get me to shut up, out of fear they would hurt me.

I catch myself. Stopping the thoughts that I'm comparing Xander to Jack. I'm not getting into a relationship with Xander. He has plenty of suitors since he's the supernatural King. He certainly wouldn't be interested in the likes of me.

So why, despite telling myself it wouldn't work out, do I find my heartrate picking up when I'm around him. Why do I find myself looking out for him? Wanting to know what he's up to. Loving when he gives me the slightest bit of attention. I feel like a teenager again with a crush.

Sue pulls me from my thoughts. "You'll be leaving with King Alexander. He requires some help from you today."

"I can't do that. I work for you Sue," I state. "I can't keep running off to do other things when I'm meant to be working here. It's not fair on you."

With a broad smile, she says, "You're right. You work for me. So, I'm ordering you to go with Xander. I'll call Melanie and ask if she's available. I'll manage, don't you worry."

Realising the truth of her words, I accept defeat and go to grab my bag. Then Xander and I leave the bakery with a couple of freshly baked treats, and we head to his sleek looking car. I'm not a car whiz, so I have no idea if it's a good one. All I know, is it's not covered in rust, muck or dints, so it's certainly healthier than any of the cars I've previously owned.

"Let's get this shit show over with," I mutter to myself, buckling my seat.

CHAPTER 19

X ander and I drive towards the estate in silence. It's awkward. Sometimes silence can be good and comfortable. Christ, I'm not usually much of a chatty Cathy, but there's too much hanging in the air. Like the overwhelming crush I have on him. Although thankfully, I don't think he's aware of that. But then there's the problem that my family are all immortals, or immortal truths, and I know that intimidates him more than he wants to admit. But the worst of all the situations hanging in the air between us, is the fact he thinks I use a gigantic dildo and don't find it uncomfortable.

"Just so you know, Melvin isn't mine," I state.

"Who's Melvin?" he asks, frowning at me.

"Shit, I forgot most men don't realise we

name sex toys," I explain. He snorts out a laugh. "Melvin is the mega-dong I smacked myself in the head with," I remark, making him laugh even more. I might as well own up to the fact that entire situation happened.

"Right," he says, struggling just to get that one word out over the laughing. "Dare I ask whose it is then?"

"Alexis'. Although you didn't hear that from me," I warn him.

"Understood." He salutes me while still maintaining focus on the road. "Why were you holding Alexis' mega-dong?"

It's my turn to laugh. I'd never have guessed that I'd hear those words come out of anyone's mouth, but especially not his.

"I took a potion meant to increase libido. It clashed with the ceremony spell, because Rose and Elana neglected to mention I should avoid any magic for a few days. Next thing I know I can speak to sex toys. To prove a point, I found Alexis' sex toys to get some information from one of them, so the girls knew I was being serious. Hence why I had hold of Melvin," I sum up for him.

In all my years I never thought I'd be having a conversation with the supernatural King about a talking mega-dong called Melvin.

He doesn't seem to know how to reply, so again we slip into even more awkward silence. If anything, it's more awkward now than it was before.

About ten minutes later, he speaks up again. "Is everything alright with your ex-husband?" he asks softly into the quiet. Something in the way he asks has me on high alert.

Heaving out a sigh, I say, "Yeah. He's just being his usual prickish self. There's a reason we divorced after all."

"Fair enough. Can't exactly judge," he replies.

"No, you can't. Did you really think sleeping with that slut was a good idea?" I ask him with amusement.

"Alright, I get it. Everyone makes mistakes," he mutters.

We lapse into silence again, only this time it's rather peaceful. I find my eyes flitting to him, checking him out through the corner of my eye. He's so hot. He seems different to pretty much everyone else I've ever met.

Staring out the window, I watch as we pass tree after tree. Despite this being a small town, it's not actually small. There aren't excessive amounts of inhabitants, only around 2,000 at most, but the land that makes up the town is a hell of a lot bigger than most would think. The estate is located further away from the main shopping area to ensure privacy for the supernaturals, which means there's a fair few miles to travel between the two places. It's what made my run to the estate before, even more surprising. Still, the beauty in being in the middle of nowhere is certainly something else I missed when I was living in the city. Now I get to enjoy it every day.

"So why have I been sent with you? What are we doing?" I ask him. Why that didn't occur to me sooner I'll never know. But I suppose it'll be best to figure out what's going on now rather than later. Although if he doesn't want to tell me, I'll soon figure out what is happening.

"We just want to try to figure out what is going on," he explains. "No one else has been attacked luckily, but it's still concerning they're out there."

Still, I'm confused why they would need me. Surely, they have supernaturals with more knowledge and training than me. I'd have thought they'd be better to have, when coming up with any sort of plans.

"Alright. But I still don't understand. Why

me?" I ask Xander again.

Out of nowhere, there's a loud bang that shakes the ground. The car goes flying and we roll end over end. With each turn of the car another part of my body is bashed, scratched or broken. It seems to go on forever.

Eventually we stop rolling with the car upside down and us hanging from our seatbelts. My head swims, and I'm almost certain I'm going to hurl. If I was to, it'd go all over. Attempting to blink away the blurry vision, I take stock of the situation. If I'm right, it was some sort of explosion rather than a crash. Nothing hit us, but we went flying.

Explosions mean a possible danger still out there. The supernatural King is in the car and there's no one here but me to protect him. Despite the pain. Despite wanting to pass out for a month, I know I have to protect him. Even if he wasn't the king, I'd protect him. He's mine.

Without allowing myself to think too much on the possessiveness that seems to plague me when it comes to him, I unclip my seatbelt. I drop onto the roof of the car and cry out at the agony that rips through my other arm, my leg, and ... well, pretty much every part of my body.

It takes a lot of effort, but I sit myself up and check in on Xander. He's unconscious and seems to have some damage done, although I have no way of knowing exactly what sort of injuries he has without him being awake.

"Xander," I call out to him. Tapping his cheek slightly to get him to wake up. When he doesn't, my blood starts pumping as ice cold fear holds me tight in its clutches. "Xander!" I call again, this time pressing my fingers to the pulse in his neck. Steady beats drum out, and I sigh in relief.

He groans and another sigh slips from me. As he wakes up, I help him unfasten his seatbelt and try to protect him when he falls, although with one arm out of commission and all the other injuries I've got, it doesn't help too much.

Whilst he's orienting himself, I attempt to escape the wreckage. First trying the door and attempting to kick it out. Pain lances up one of my legs, and I scream. Fuck, I'm pretty sure it's broken. Instead, I aim at the already smashed front window, using my good arm to make a big enough gap to drag myself through.

Once out, I grab a hold of Xanders arm and, stood only on one leg, heave him through. I land on my arse but he's at least out of the wreckage. We need to call for backup.

Feeling in my pockets for my phone, I pull out what remains. Fuck. It doesn't work, which isn't surprising since half of it is missing. I've no idea where the other half is, although even if I did it wouldn't make my phone work.

"Where's your phone?" I ask Xander.

A loud bellow or possibly a growl, a mixture of both would be more accurate, rips through the area, and I whip my head up. I recognise that sound. For fucks sake.

With Xander still on the ground, too dazed to be of any help, I know it's down to me. A wraith bite won't kill me, but it'd kill Xander, and I can't let that happen.

Wraiths start to close in around us and I have no idea what to do.

"Weapon. I need a weapon," I say to myself. Somehow speaking out loud helps me to organise my thoughts and get myself into action.

Scanning the ground, I find a piece of broken metal. It's got a jagged enough edge to cause some serious damage, not only to the wraiths, but also to my hand, but it's the best I can do. I've not got much hope for being able to fend all the creatures off, but I have to try. I'll also have to try and do it while only using one leg and one arm.

I hold up my makeshift weapon to the wraiths. There are three of them. Without warning they swarm in. Before I know what's happened, three wraiths surround me, swiping, clawing, and biting at me from all angles. I slice repeatedly into any bit of skin I can reach. Tearing and hacking into flesh as screams of agony rip from me.

A wraith bites into my shoulder from behind and I stab my weapon over my shoulder. It sinks into flesh with a sickening squelch. When I pull the metal out the wraith slumps to the ground unresponsive. It would seem head shots destroy them. So that's what I aim for with the other two. I sink the weapon into the second one's skull. It drops to the ground.

Before I can strike the third one, It grabs a hold of me. Claws tear into my gut, and teeth sink into the same side of my neck as the first one. Only this time the creature pulls, taking my flesh with him. My voice goes hoarse from screaming so much, but I pull up enough energy to sink the blade into the wraith, dropping it to the ground.

With the enemy destroyed, my energy fades leaving me shaking and disoriented. Hobbling to Xander, who finally seems to be more aware of his surroundings, I ask, "Do you have your phone?"

He looks up at me horror-stricken. "Are you alright?"

What a stupid fucking question to ask! "Do you have your phone?" I repeat.

Xander pats at his pockets in a similar way to what I did. He pulls a battered and broken phone from his pocket, and I curse. Slumping to the ground, I struggle not to cry. I'm not one to cry often, but in situations like this it's incredibly hard not to.

What the hell are we meant to do now? Neither of us are in too good of a position to go anywhere but staying here and waiting for someone to find us, could lead to our deaths. We were attacked once, it's not improbable for someone to come and check to see if the wraiths did their jobs of finishing us off.

Drawing up non-existent energy, I sit myself up.

"We need to get out of the open," I state to Xander, who seems to be just as drained as I am.

"Can you even walk?" he asks me. "Also, you never answered my question. Are you alright?"

"I can hop," I remark, since walking isn't really in the cards right now. "I'm pretty sure my leg and arm are broken. My shoulder has been torn up, and I have too many injuries to count. No, I'm not alright, but the only way either of us are getting help is if we go to the estate."

He seems to register the truth of my words and nods his head.

"Are you alright?" I ask, realising I still don't know what injuries he possibly has.

"Think I hit my head pretty hard because my eyesight is rather blurred. Can't really see much if I'm honest, but other than that, and full body bruising, I'm alright. I'll help you walk but you'll have to lead us," he chuckles. "Talk about blind leading the blind!"

True to his word, he needed my help to navigate the woods. We both figured that despite the difficulty in walking on the uneven ground, it's too dangerous to remain in the open, so instead we stick to the trees. I lead him, making sure he's aware of any large obstacles in his way. He supports me with my good arm thrown over his shoulder and taking a lot of my weight, making it easier for me to hop along with him.

The progress is slow, but with each hour that passes his eyesight gets marginally better. Me on the other hand, I feel more and more drained, like someone is literally leeching the energy from my body.

Xander trips on a log he didn't see and that I'd missed in my tiredness. We both go crashing down into the twigs and leaves that litter the ground. The jolting pain makes my breath catch, and before I know it, I'm out for the count and darkness swallows me whole.

CHAPTER 20

The following morning, I wake with a groan. Every part of my body is stiff as a board. Worse, I feel sick to my stomach. Without even being able to move from my prone position on the floor, vomit rises up and pours out of my mouth. Being too weak to move, I just lie there as I continue expelling the contents of my stomach.

"Freyja," Xander calls out, sounding worried.

Why does he always seem so worried around me? Believe it or not, I never used to cause such panic in people. Despite me being arrested all the time, people knew I could take care of myself, so just let me get on with my life. But poor Xander is going to make himself ill if he carries on fretting like a mother hen.

I don't see Xander move, but I'm lifted gently from the ground, and he manoeuvres me to help me sit and throw up properly. He probably doesn't want me choking on my own puke, which, I'm ashamed to say, is a large possibility.

With my stomach once again empty, he lifts me into his arms and carries me from the sight.

"We need to get you back to the estate," Xander states.

"Well done, captain obvious," I joke weakly.

"You look half dead and you're still joking. Maybe it's not as bad as we think," he offers, as he scoops me into his arms like I weigh nothing.

"Only half dead? Feel worse than that," I joke.

Despite my exhaustion and the pain rippling through me, I can't sleep. Every little movement hurts, but my body doesn't switch off and allow me the blessed relief of unconsciousness. So instead, I lightly doze on Xander, and shake from the pain. He holds onto me for dear life. Despite everything, I love being in his arms. Being able to listen to the steady thump of his heart.

"How's your sight?" I ask him, only just remembering he'd had a knock to the head.

"Still fuzzy, but clearer than it was," he offers, and the selfish part of me just prays he doesn't trip over again.

The idea of suffering more injuries on top of how shit I'm already feeling, makes me shake even worse. Yes, it's selfish, but you'd probably be thinking the same thing in my position.

"Supernaturals really do heal quicker," I remark, kind of impressed his vision is already getting better.

If he was human, that bump to his head could have left him with permanent sight problems. Then again if we were human, we would have likely both died in that accident. It wasn't exactly a small one, and I'm pretty sure we've both lost enough blood, or sustained enough damage, to kill a human.

"I'm more worried as to why you're not healing very quickly," Xander states. "In fact, you're still losing a fair amount of blood. Although, I suppose it's a good sign that you're transitioning, as it would seem your blood is replicating quicker than it should," he explains.

Huh, I didn't even realise that was a thing. Then again with how hardy supernaturals are, and the fact it's incredibly difficult to kill us, I suppose it would make some sense.

"That being said your magic is being

drained working so hard to constantly replenish it, which is likely why you're so tired. Plus, you're trying to heal multiple injuries. Your magic is probably getting tapped out too quickly to heal everything, so focuses on your blood, not realising you need your wounds closing for that to be affective," he says out loud. I realise he's not so much talking to me, but instead trying to ease his worries about why I'm not healing like he is.

We stop for a few minutes, and he sets me down on the ground. I lay down not even having the energy to sit up. Tearing strips off his shirt, Xander works to stop the flow of blood escaping from the shoulder, since that's the main cause of the blood loss. It hurts like a bitch, and I scream as he tightens the cloth around it to apply pressure. Despite the pain, I know he's only trying to help me. With that sorted, he lifts me back up and we continue our journey to the estate.

We seem to travel for hours, although with me lightly dozing along the way, I have no real way to judge how long it's actually been. But finally, we make it to the estate. Walking up to the gates, Xander orders them to be opened. As soon as the guards securing the perimeter see us, they rush over.

Obviously, their aim is to ensure the kings safety and check he is alright, but he's more concerned about me. Being only partially aware of my surroundings, I don't understand who's trying to take me from Xander. My arms grip him tighter, refusing to let him go. I'm worse than a baby monkey with it's mother.

"Honey, you need to let him go. He's been carrying you a while and he needs medical care as well," I hear my grandfather explaining.

Releasing my hold on Xander, I'm handed over to Papi. Knowing it's him, I settle and carry on my light dozing. The steady thump of his heart lulls me into calmness as he carries me carefully towards the infirmary.

I hear Xander informing the guards of what occurred.

"She saved my life," Xander adds in adoration, when they questioned how we escaped the wraiths.

I didn't expect such wonder in his voice. It's as though he couldn't believe I'd put myself in front of him, to protect him. As though he couldn't believe I would die to protect him, and that was a massive possibility.

"She will. We may make fun of her for ending up in trouble. But it was always in defence of another, which is why she was never charged," my Papi explains. "She's vicious. But above all else she is a protector."

"I'm starting to see that," he says softly.

"No," I say weakly. "I'm a nasty violent woman. Ain't no one going to call me a protector." I joke with them. It's not the first time someone's called me that, but what they don't realise is that I've often struggled to restrain myself. Often, I don't just want to subdue someone, I want to kill them.

Xander and my Papi laugh at that. Once we make it to the healers, I'm laid gently on one of the beds.

"I feel like I should just assign you your own bed missy," the healer says, coming over to me.

"Probably. Although I'm blaming you guys for this. I've never needed to go to the hospital so often," I explain.

My shirt is cut from my body. Since it's only Papi, a few healers, and Xander in the room, I'm not bothered by anyone seeing me naked. I'm pretty sure Xander has already seen me at least partially undressed, but for some reason, I'm even more reluctant to leave his side. I've only known the hotty for a short time, but I'm infatuated with him. Every time he enters a room my heart skips a beat, and he drags all my focus to him. Obviously instead of showing that attraction, I rip into him, but I'm pretty sure my family know the truth. After all, they know very well that my love language is sarcasm.

Once I'm undressed, the healer orders for some water and a flannel to be bought over. She washes me down to get a clearer sight on my injuries starting with my shoulder. I cry out and she apologises to me, although she carries on cleaning it.

Xander jumps up and rushes over, ignoring the healer seeing to him.

"Don't hurt her," he warns the healer tending to me.

"Sit your arse down dickhead," I order Xander. "It'll hurt, but it's for the best."

He looks to me, then to the healer. But the most shocking thing is the look on my Papi's face. He's staring at Xander in shock and surprise, but it starts morphing into amusement.

"She's your...," Papi cuts himself off, bursts out laughing, and continues to do so until tears are streaming down his face. "Oh, you poor, poor man," he mutters, shaking his head in disbelief.

"Miss, can you smack him," I ask the healer, indicating my Papi. "I would do it myself, but I don't think I can even lift this battered thing at the moment," I explain.

I'm surprised when she listens to me and

smacks my Papi around the head. She doesn't do it lightly either. It was my understanding that people revere my Papi, and ..., well ..., most of my family, for being immortal truths. But the healer lets her hand fly without any concern as to the repercussions. It's my turn to laugh, especially when my Papi and Xander look to the healer in surprise. Us women stick together apparently.

"You, shut the fuck up. If you stay in here, you sit down, shut up and stay out of our way," the healer orders my Papi, who actually follows her instructions. "And you," she points to Xander, "get your arse back in that bed, and allow Healer Ryan to check you over. Just because you heal quickly, doesn't mean it will heal correctly," she orders. Again, I'm shocked when Xander listens to her, and sits himself back on the bed besides mine, allowing Healer Ryan to check on his injuries.

The healer looks me over and sighs her dismay. Seems it's worse than I thought. I don't think I'm going to drop dead anytime soon, but her look of dismay makes me think it's a possibility.

"What's the prognosis doc?" I ask her.

Despite everything, I'm still conscious, and that in itself is a bloody miracle. Or a curse. Every time they manoeuvre my body, I hurt. Every time they apply treatment or probe it, I hurt.

"Broken arm in three places. Broken leg in one place. Your shoulder is obviously torn to shreds. You've got glass stuck in your arse, although pretty sure you didn't notice that," she states, and I gawk at her. Why do I get the feeling she hasn't even finished listing my injuries.

"Hey, now we know what's up with your attitude. You've got something lodged in your arse," Xander says, much to my surprise. He's certainly getting braver.

"I may be battered to hell, but I can still beat you into next week if you start that shit," I warn him.

"Anyway...," the healer states, drawing my attention to her. "You've got two broken ribs, glass stuck in your legs, you're suffering catastrophic blood loss, and I'm honestly surprised you are even conscious," she explains. I suppose that's never a promising thing to be told. Catastrophic blood loss sounds like a serious thing. "Your magic is replenishing your blood but is draining itself doing that and is unable to close the wounds at the same time. Despite you being supernatural you are still in transition which is why you aren't healing as you should. You have a limited supply of magic within you, until you transition fully," she explains to me.

I'm thankful she does, because I wouldn't have had any clue what she meant otherwise. Being new to the supernatural world is a struggle. Having to learn everything in such a short time is difficult. Even more so as we have a current threat, that is forcing me to figure it all out quicker than most would have to.

"Should I pay for my funeral now?" I ask light-heartedly.

"In most instances, I'd say yes. But I think it's safe to say you're not going to die anytime soon, or you would've already been dead," she deadpans, and I hear a choked sound coming from Papi. I suppose the news that if I was more human, I'd be dead, is an awful thought for him to consider. Especially since I'm his only grandbaby, and obviously even if I wasn't his only one, I'd still be his favourite.

"On a positive note, we will do surgery to repair some of the damage to stop the catastrophic blood loss. We will splint your arm and leg to ensure they stay in the right position, and obviously check to make sure they're in the right places. Then your body should heal itself within a couple of weeks. You will have scarring, but I get the feeling that wouldn't bother you," the healer states.

She's got a point. After that I'm given a

sedative, so they can get to work putting my broken body back together.

CHAPTER 21

I wake to an incessant beeping. With the dregs of sleep still clinging to me, I attempt to hit my phone to shut it up. When my hand sails through thin air, I realise what happened. Blinking away the sleep, I open my eyes to the bright florescent lights of the infirmary. For fucks sake.

"Good afternoon, Freyja, I'm glad to see you're awake," the healer from before states, coming over to me.

She adjusts the bed to help me sit up, which gives me a good chance to take everything in. My arm is in a cast along with my leg. The shoulder that had been torn up feels like it has been stitched in some places before a thick sturdy dressing had been applied. Judging by the way the healer manoeuvres my arm to rest on a pillow, my guess is she doesn't want me moving it too much.

"What's your name?" I ask, realising I still don't know it, despite how often I'm here.

Then again, considering when I'm here I'm usually out of it, I suppose it's to be expected. Still, I feel quite rude not knowing the name of the woman who is constantly patching me up when I make bad decisions.

She chuckles. "I'm Healer Rosa Delacroix," she offers.

"Well Healer Rosa, when can I escape my prison?" I ask with a bright smile.

It isn't her who responds. "I'd have thought you'd know the difference between prison and an infirmary Jailbird," Xander says, and I growl at him. He only smiles.

"Now now kids. Settle down," Healer Rosa orders. "You are free to leave when you want Freyja, but you need to wear this sling and avoid putting weight on your leg," she explains.

She helps me put on a sling that not only elevates my broken arm, but also ensures my injured shoulder stays immobilised. Just as I assumed would be the case. She brings over a wheelchair for me to sit in, and I look at her in annoyance. I'm not getting in that. Don't get me wrong, there's nothing wrong with a wheelchair if you need it. But I can manage without. I don't need people pushing me around and tending to me.

"Sit in the chair," the Healer hisses and her fangs slip out in annoyance. So, I was right after all, she's a vampire. I'm actually shocked that the kind and caring woman can display any anger or sternness. It doesn't work on me, but it's still surprising.

"Any relation to Alexis?" I ask her. The resemblance between the pair is astonishing and I'm certain there's a connection. She's also on the right side of nutty to not fear me, which so far, only Alexis is. Obviously, Rose, Elana and Jill don't fear me, but I know that their natures will bow to my power. Alexis doesn't. She may be surprised but she doesn't bow down to my power. It's also not because her power level is on par with mine. It's just because she's nutty as hell.

"She's my daughter," Rosa states, and I can suddenly see it perfectly.

It would also explain the stern behaviour. If Alexis is her daughter, she'd have had to master the parental punishment early on.

I follow her orders, and slowly get up to sit in the wheelchair. I offer my thanks to her for fixing me up. Before I leave, she gives me orders to return in two days, so she can check on my healing.

Since I'm transitioning, there's no way of telling how long it will take me to heal. It could take two days, or it could take two weeks. If I suddenly finish transitioning in the next day, there's a good chance I'd have finished healing within the two-day time frame. The check is just to ensure everything is moving along nicely.

As soon as Xander has pushed my wheelchair out of the infirmary, I stop him. Then I carefully lift myself up until I'm standing.

"Jailbait, get back in the wheelchair," Xander orders.

Instead of answering, I hobble my way to the lift at the end of the hallway. Since Healer Rosa isn't here to go all motherly judgement on me, I'm not going to sit in that damn chair. I need to move.

Xander grumbles a complaint but follows along with the wheelchair. Once in the lift he pushes the button for the 5th floor. We ride in silence. When the door opens, I hobble my way out and give everything a good look.

I recognise this floor as the one that contains Xander's office. It wasn't that long ago I was here beating up Lucifer. The memory makes me smile. Xander had gotten so angry at me for beating, physically and verbally, the immortal truths. Now he knows the truth and he probably regret's trying to stop me. I'd have probably done him a favour knocking my parents and Uncle Lucifer down a few pegs.

"Where are we going?" I ask Xander.

The fact he's chosen the floor with his office, suggests he has a plan that doesn't include me sleeping for a week.

"Command centre," he states, taking the lead and walking towards the direction of his office.

He doesn't go to his office though, and instead holds a door open for me to the right of his office. Entering the room, I gape at the sight. Large screens cover most of the wall space in the room. In the centre of the room is a large table that is covered in all sorts of papers. It's an honest to god war room. It's amazing.

Without meaning to, a squeal escapes me. My parents and grandparents both shake their heads in amusement, and I spot Alexis and Jillian at the computers trying not to laugh.

"Note to self. To impress Freyja take her to a command centre," Xander mutters.

Something about his comment has me quirking a brow at him. Why would he be trying to impress me? I thought he couldn't stand me. Then again, I suppose I also give him that impression with my bad attitude and jabbing.

"Can't say any of the women I've been with have been impressed by such a thing," Xander adds, and I growl.

Who the hell has he been dating? He's mine.

Again, I have to shake away those possessive thoughts. What the actual fuck is wrong with me? He's not mine. We hate each other. That's right, we hate each other. I need to keep saying that. Maybe eventually I'll even start to believe it.

"Holy shit," Gigi gasps. "You're mates," Gigi adds, looking between Xander and me in amazement.

What the hell are mates? Does she mean friends? I've always hated that term. Why can't people just say friends. Mate is such a dickish word.

"I can promise you, we aren't friends," I state to my grandmother. "If anything, we're arch nemeses," I add.

"Keep telling yourself that dear. No one believes you," she states, grinning like a Cheshire cat at me.

Deciding to change the topic, I ask, "Why are we here? Has something happened? Do I need to go get my mace?"

The people manning the computers turn to look at me in question. Clearly, they think that just because I'm injured, I'll be useless. They couldn't be more wrong.

"No little devil spawn niece," Lucifer trills, coming over to pick me up.

"Put me down shithead," I order, and he cackles as he sets me on a chair.

"Stay," he orders tapping my nose.

When he turns around, I kick out my good leg aiming right between his own legs. I connect to my mark. Much to my delight a kick to the balls has the same effect on him as it does all other males. Lucifer cups his injured genitals and braces himself on the table as he rides the waves of pain.

Much to my delight, I see a few of the women in the room chuckling at my attack. The men on the other hand wince in sympathy, cupping their own genitals as though they're experiencing sympathy pains. But once they realise, I just took down the devil with ease, they get back to work. Clearly, they've learnt I'm still deadly, even when injured.

"Calm down," Xander grumbles, deciding to ignore my assault on the devil. Huh, he's learning. "Nothing has happened, other than us being attacked. That being said, we have a feeling the attack wasn't aimed at me, but at you," he explains.

My mind promptly fizzles. Somehow, I can work with others being attacked and me being the one to guard them. But me being the one in danger and others protecting me? Yeah, that doesn't sit well with me. I'd prefer to protect myself.

"Ah, look at you." Lucifer giggles. Clearly, he's recovered. "Too stunned to speak. Who did you piss off to warrant a death sentence?" he adds. When I make a move to kick him again, he practically jumps into my father's arms. My dad merely drops him to the ground and kicks him himself.

"You think I'm the one being targeted?" I ask for clarification.

"Yes," my grandfather states.

Well, if no one else has been attacked, while I've been attacked three times, I can understand their thought process.

"For fucks sake," I growl. "But why me. The attacks started after I moved here, and I haven't been here long enough to create enemies."

Everyone, and I mean everyone, in the room quirks their brow at me. Oh yeah, Karen. I hadn't even made it to the town before making an enemy.

"We need to know of anyone who'd have it out for you," my mother states.

"Probably easier to get a list of those she hasn't pissed off," Lucifer snorts.

I mean he has a point. I'm not exactly the nicest of people. I also have a habit of speaking with my fists. Or a foot, as he learnt.

I try to come up with a list in my mind of all the people who could possibly have it out for me. True to the devils' predictions it's quite a long one. Instead of thinking about small grievances though, I consider the ones close to the situation at hand. Someone magical for starters. Or someone with knowledge of the supernatural. Problem is, is that I don't know who is and isn't magical.

"Karen would be a high probability," I start.

"She's a banshee," Xander explains, biting his lip. "It's at least a possibility, but it seems extreme for her to attack in such a way, especially since you were a human when you were first attacked."

So not Karen then.

"Obviously my ex would be a big possibility, but he doesn't know of supernaturals," I explain.

It's true. He's the sort of person who won't even read a fantasy book because he finds it too unrealistic. I've no idea what the hell is wrong with him, and I'm honestly questioning why I ever married the damn fucker.

"What about those you had grievances with before you left?" Xander asks.

This time I see my parents and grandparents' wince. I also spot Jillian at one of the computers and she pauses in her work. Alexis seems just as confused as I am by everyone's strange behaviour.

They know something I don't.

"I don't remember much from when I left," I state, watching my family closely. Again, they wince and look away slightly.

Didn't Mark say something about compulsion being used to get me out of town. Surely that wouldn't be the reason I'm struggling to remember. That was only to get me out of the town.

They know why I can't remember much. I'm sure of it. But if they know, that means they played a role in it all. Maybe they're the ones responsible. Now that I've been back for a bit, I've realised just how many blank spaces there are in my memories. The incident was the last thing of this place I remember, but there are a few days in between that and me leaving, that I also don't remember.

"What aren't you telling me?" I ask my family. "Don't try to lie to me," I growl out, knowing that is exactly what they will do.

"You didn't leave because of the incident," my mum heaves out.

"No, I left because I was compelled to leave," I state. That's what Mark had said, right?

A cold feeling drips through me as my heart rate increases with my anger. They know why I left, and I get the feeling they know more about it than what Mark had told me. He just said I was compelled to leave because it wasn't safe for a human.

"You know more than you're letting on. Explain," I clench out.

CHAPTER 22

My blood seems to boil in my veins as this new betrayal comes to light. Not only did my family fake their own death, but they played a role in me leaving my home and not wanting to come back. Who the fuck does that to their child? Worse, they seem to be under the impression that the incident isn't what caused me to leave the town in the first place? Surely that did in fact happen.

I've been saying for some time it makes no sense that that would be the reason to keep me away for so long, especially since I'm over it. Yet that was always the response I'd give people when they asked why I wouldn't go back. What the hell is going on? And why are my family looking at me as though they're expecting me to blow up? Could this be worse than the incident?

"Tell me what the fuck is going on," I scream at my family.

It's Jillian who speaks up. She wrings her hands, a clear show of her nerves. "By the age of 18 those who are supernatural typically show their powers," she starts. "You hadn't. You were human. But everyone around you was supernatural, and the law states that humans can't know about us. Not even supernatural with children are allowed to divulge the information to their children. There are instances where it's allowed but that's for another conversation," Jill starts to ramble.

My anger slowly starts to calm, only slightly. That makes sense. They're just trying to protect the information, although personally I wouldn't make the law allow for such a secret to be kept around their own children. What is the harm in children knowing their parents, even the supernatural side of them, whether they end up supernatural or human?

"A test was devised. If you reacted to it, you were human and wasn't allowed to stay. If you didn't react than you had a supernatural side that would emerge," Jill explains, and the realisation of what she is implying, startles me.

They tested me in some way, and I failed.

"How did you test me?" I ask, dreading the

answer.

"I tried to get them to not do it. I told them it would be a terrible idea. But it was decreed by the royals a long time ago that we had to test you. This was deemed the safest of all the options," Jill rambles, clearly uncomfortable with whatever she knows.

I try to think of all the times I could possibly have been tested. I've got blanks in some places, but for the most part it's only surrounding me leaving that I can't remember. The last memory that sticks out is... that night.

The colour seems to drain from my face as I realise exactly what she's talking about. There's no way that that was the safest option.

"You spiked my drink," I state, rather than question.

That night I had gone out with, who at the time was my boyfriend, Dane. Jill was with us along with a couple of other school friends. My parents and grandparents had stayed at home, but now that I think about it, they had seemed rather clingy. They kept hugging me and telling me how much they loved me. I thought it was just because it was my birthday, and I was now legally an adult. But that wasn't it at all.

"A vampire needed to be there," my mother fills in. "The only one close to you was 'him'," she explains, not using his name. Likely knowing how I would react. Although just like the incident itself, I have no idea why I react so poorly to the name.

"We made sure your friends where there as well to ensure nothing happened to you. We tried to protect you as much as we could," my mother continues. Tears start falling down her face as she recounts what they had done.

"So you spiked my drink with a drug that is very similar, if not the same, as what humans do on nights out when they want their victim pliant and unconscious?" I state in disbelief. How was that a good choice?

"You never got ill. Never had problems healing injuries. You had the same resilience to human medications as the supernatural," my dad tries to explain. "It was obvious that some of our supernatural genetics got passed down, but that doesn't make you supernatural. There are only a handful of drugs that we can test with, to know for certain. That was the least harmful one," he tries to explain. "Supernaturals don't react to it at all. We never have. It's all about our magic attacking it. Our magic doesn't attack medications in quite the same way, but it does burn out of our systems quicker. It was the best way to test you without you realising it was a test," he explains it to me.

I know from recent experience that our bodies burn off human medications a lot quicker than humans. It's part of the reason they use potions when possible. A supernatural would burn the drug out of their system before it took effect. For someone who doesn't have magic backing up their system, it wouldn't burn out quick enough and would affect a person.

"So, you got 'him' to drug me, and what..." I ask.

My mind tries to figure out what I've read about vampires. They're fast, strong and drink blood. But what else can they do that would make them necessary for that specific task.

"Mind control?" I state. "He controlled my mind, or something, didn't he? Made me leave because I wasn't supernatural."

My parents and grandparents nod their heads in confirmation.

"It's called compulsion," Gigi explains.

"So, he compelled me to leave my home. My family. My friends. Everyone I knew," I start, and my voice rises with my anger. "You let them kick me from my home, and didn't even fight it," I ask in disbelief.

My parents are crying by this point. Jillian is shaking as racking sobs pour from her. Alexis comforts her. But all I can think is that they all act sad about this, but they didn't have to live with getting kicked from their own home, and having to move to a place where you know no one. Everything was different and I had to just make it. They barely ever called, and my family never visited. Only Jill met up with me.

"Did it ever occur to you that maybe I was just a late bloomer. You said it yourself. Only typically people show their magic by 18. I could resist certain medications; I could access the estate which is apparently warded to keep humans out. But you still insisted on doing this horrific thing. The one incident I remember is that…" I scream at them. Then something occurs to me. I remember the incident. Surely, if I was truly affected by it, I wouldn't have remembered. That's one of the problems with it. "How do I remember the incident if it affected me so well," I ask.

"Freyja," Xander speaks softly. "Don't go too hard on them," he adds, without answering my questions.

My furious glare turns his way. "Don't fucking touch me," I growl at him. "It's your family that made this a fucking law. In fact, you were the one ruling at the time this was enacted. Why the hell would you have such a monstrous rule?" I ask.

I don't even realise I'm crying until a tear drip's from my cheek and lands on my hand. The betrayal I feel is worse than anything I've ever experienced before in my life. How could anyone think that this was an acceptable thing to do?

"Sir you called for me," a mans voice breaks the tense silence.

"Yes, could you help your sister in looking for Freyja's school records please," Xander states to the new person. It's like he's trying to draw away from the conversation at hand.

I get the feeling he's hoping that a distraction will take from the current events playing out. He should know it isn't going to work and he's an idiot for thinking that.

The man who entered goes over to Alexis. Huh, I didn't know she had a sibling. He's similar to her with the same fiery red hair and lithe frame, although he's certainly a bit taller than her petite height.

Trying to draw myself away from all the betrayal, I ask, "is it possible 'he' is the one wanting some kind of revenge. I'm sure knowing I'm back would be a pretty terrifying experience for 'him'," I ask the room.

They give one another a side eye. Jillian is nervously glancing to her right. At the man who entered. They couldn't possibly be suggesting, what I think they're suggesting.

"Who is this guy?" Alexis asks.

Looking to her, I can't help noticing her brother beside her. He hasn't turned around, but his hands have stilled on the keyboard.

"What's your brother called?" I ask. Getting the impression that I already know. Please don't say Dane. Please don't say it.

"Dane," she responds, and the fury that was already at a rolling boil, bubbles over.

All I see is red. Ignoring my injuries, I jump up and grab a hold of the man. Alexis screams, but I ignore her focusing on the face of the one person I never wanted to see again. It's only when I see him fully, that I learn something even more startling. He's the one who helped me that night. That's how he knew I'd be good with a mace. I'd spent years training with him.

We used to train with my Papi often. Sometimes if my family were busy, we'd train together. He'd always found it amusing that I used melee weapons over the typical blades or bow and arrows.

My fist slams into the desk behind him. Knowing he's Alexis' brother and that he did save me, is the only thing stopping me from killing the prick. I get the feeling he was as much of a pawn in this situation as I was. But it still doesn't take away from the fact that my mind is insisting I destroy him.

Before I know it, I start punching and smashing everything in sight. My anger, my hurt and the betrayal all fly from me in a fury.

My shoulder screams in pain, as does my leg and arm, but I can't stop myself. It's like all my anger has just boiled over and I'm incapable of stopping it or reining it back in.

Most of those in the room flee, as my outburst leads me to throwing anything and everything.

The table gets smashed. The computers get thrown.

My family abandoned me. I was tested with a date-rape drug. I was compelled. They all fucking knew. They faked their own fucking deaths.

"Fucking pricks," I scream, picking up a chair and throwing it at the wall. It hits and sinks into the wall enough that I suspect it sticks out the other side.

Tears blur my vision, but the betrayal keeps fuelling the fire filling my veins.

All these years I believed that the incident was the reason I had left the town. The reason

I'd left my home. But it wasn't. That entire incident was staged to test me. All my friends and family went along with it and tested me in such a horrific way, all to check I was supernatural. They never once thought that maybe I was just a late bloomer or showing my abilities in different ways. Worse, once I was booted out, they didn't bother visiting or calling and just decided to fake their own fucking deaths. Would Jill have done the same soon, if I didn't show any abilities?

I don't know how much time passes, but eventually my energy and anger fade. Sinking to the ground, I sob. My heart feels like it's been ripped out of my chest.

How could they do this to me?

CHAPTER 23

L aying in one of the guest rooms, I feel drained. Everything hurts, not only physically but emotionally.

When I'd first left..., I suppose I was forced out..., I'd felt alone. My mind had been running through what I should do now, knowing that I didn't have my family or friends to turn to. I'd left and seemed to float in uncertainty for a while.

I'd never wanted to feel that lost again. But that's exactly how I feel. Everyone of meaning in my life has betrayed and hurt me, and I don't know how to get through it.

After my outburst in the command centre, I'd fallen asleep on the ground. Healer Rosa had come in, and I'd pulled away from the mother of the man who compelled and drugged me. She'd ended up asking me if I wanted a sedative.

Knowing I'd undone all her hard work in patching me up, and the fact I was still a mess, I'd agreed.

When I had awoken, I was in this bed. My wounds had been dressed and cleaned. A note on my bedside table told me I'd nearly completed my transition, so my wounds where healing quicker than predicted. That should be good news, but I feel like my outside should hurt as much as my insides. As much as my heart and mind hurt.

I'd always just remembered the incident, and then the next thing I knew I was moving into a flat in the city. Even to this day I don't recall driving to the city, or having my things moved. It's like I was just placed on the doorstep of the flat and that was it. I'm not sure if that was part of the compulsion, or whether it was the shock of everything happening.

But the day I'd moved into the flat, the first thing I did was sit on the sofa and sob. I sobbed for hours and hours until I'd fallen asleep. Knowing I went through all that because of my family, doesn't make this current situation any easier to deal with.

A knock on the door pulls me from my own thoughts. It's pushed open slightly and Gigi pokes her head inside. She has bags under her red rimmed eyes. She's been crying. It would seem this entire incident has had us all feeling upset and hurt. The bitchy side of me wonders what she has to cry about. She's one of the people who could have prevented it all in the first place. But she didn't.

"May I come in?" she asks.

"Sure. I'm sure you'd just get Dane to compel me if I don't," I remark. Part of me regrets it the moment I see the hurt in her face. Something I've never seen before. But at the same time, I'm glad she hurts even slightly as much as I do.

"Do you know what can happen to all supernaturals if humans were to find out about us?" she asks, as she takes a seat on the bed. She's careful not to touch me. I only allow contact with a small group of people and I'm not always receptive to it. She still knows me well if she's careful not to touch me.

"I've read books. Of course I know. Things could go great, or supernaturals could end up experimented on, or hunted down like the witch trials," I remark. All fiction basically tells of one of those outcomes.

"So, you understand the law that states humans aren't to find out about us?" she asks.

"Obviously I understand it," I offer, getting irritated. "But that doesn't mean you had to force me out. I was part of the supernatural community, even if I wasn't aware of it. My entire family are supernatural. There was no need to kick me out," I explain.

"Our town is moving in the direction of being supernatural only. That includes a ward to keep out humans," she adds. "Look, just know it was incredibly difficult for us to do this. I'm Mother Nature and even I couldn't prevent this from needing to happen."

She seems to genuinely believe this. But I can't understand why the being, who is essentially the beginning of all life, couldn't prevent her granddaughter from being booted from a small town.

"Look the law is the law. We all follow it because we all agreed to it. It was necessary for the protection of all supernaturals," she explains. "I understand you are hurt, and you feel betrayed, but just know that the reason we never visited was because it was too difficult for us to. We faked our deaths hoping to allow you the freedom to move on and cut all ties to this place. It was also needed because humans age exponentially, and despite being able to control our aging, it would have left you feeling upset that you haven't visited. We hoped it would be for the best."

I consider what she's saying. Earlier I was so caught up in how all this affected me, that I didn't consider how this affected them.

"We had you compelled to leave this town. But we put conditions in place. If at any point you needed a place to turn to, you'd come home. If your supernatural side started to arrive, you'd be drawn back home," she explains.

At least that's something. But how do I just forget about everything that's happened? How do I forget that my family and friends lied and betrayed me?

"Do you know what a benefit of being an Immortal Truth is?" Gigi asks. I shake my head. "We can exist wherever we want. Just because you were compelled to stay away, it doesn't mean we stayed away from you. All those years you were away, we would routinely check on you. We never visited as we are now, but that doesn't mean we didn't watch over you."

I try to see things from their perspective. They had to let their baby girl go into the city without them. They had to watch as the decision for me to be tested, was taken out of their hands. I can understand them being forced to follow the rules that they themselves had agreed to. It would certainly set a bad impression if they excused themselves of the rules. In fact, if I saw that happening, I'd be furious.

They knew it had to be done. That I had to

be tested. But they made sure it was the safest of the possible options. They also ensured that I was protected throughout the entire situation.

"Why did you create the law?" I ask Gigi, getting an idea of why.

"Supernaturals are very violent by nature. It was designed to protect both supernaturals and humans," she explains.

"To protect humans from the deadly nature of supernaturals. To protect supernaturals from human's fear and judgment," I state.

With each puzzle piece that fits into place, I get a better idea of why everything happened.

Humans are in danger living among supernaturals because every encounter can turn deadly. Supernaturals are quicker than humans and that speed can pose a threat. Supernaturals are strong, which can pose a threat to humans. Christ, even a lot of supernaturals dietary requirements can pose a threat to humans.

I hate the entire situation but now that I'm able to think clearer, I can understand why it had to happen.

"Okay. I get it. No one is to blame," I state, and I truly mean it.

Gigi breathes a sigh of relief and I smile at her.

"Out of curiosity, how did I manage to access the estate as a child? It's warded from humans," I ask. It's one of those things that has been festering in my mind.

"We've no idea. Realistically, if you can pass through the wards then you should have passed the test," she explains. "It's a sign that enough of your genetics are supernatural."

"But if I'm supernatural now, then why did I fail the test in the first place?" I ask.

She frowns. It's as though I can see the gears in her mind grinding away. "I've no idea. We've used that test method before and it's never let us down," she says.

"I also remember the incident. Isn't one of the characteristics of that specific drug, that you don't often remember the incident?" I ask.

Her frown deepens. "That's true. That's partially the reason we use that specific one a lot for the test. It leaves little damage since when you wake up you are uninjured and safe. Unlike when the despicable humans use it," she growls at the end.

It's part of the reason I hate people so much. Animals are the best. People are the worst.

"But that night you appeared unconscious," Gigi explains. "I don't understand how you can remember it. You had your eyes open, but you weren't tracking movement and your heartrate was steady. We thought you were asleep. When Jill had returned from her visit with you, she'd mentioned you saying about the 'incident'. We'd found it strange. But we also didn't want to interrupt your life, so we rolled with it. I suppose none of us truly thought too much of it, but now that you've brought it up, I wonder if something went wrong that night."

Despite the barrage of questions, I'm desperate to ask, I'm also too drained for that just yet. Instead, I change the topic.

"Get Papi, mum, dad and Jill, will you. We need to watch a movie and I hurt too much to move," I order, wanting to move on from all the hurt and upset.

Her smile turns to a grin as she bounces up and opens the door, revealing the culprits standing outside. Lucifer is also with them, and I roll my eyes.

I don't think I've ever truly realised just how much they love me. I've never seen how much they care for me and want the best for me. Or at least I was too oblivious to the fact.

The fact they were so concerned about me, that they actually waited outside my room wanting to know how I was.

They file into the room and we somehow all manage to squeeze onto the bed. Lucifer decides to shift into a feline, and I had no idea he could even do that. Still, I'm not entirely bothered when he curls up on my knee and lets me pet him. He's really cute with fully black fur, that's super soft. Which is probably the weirdest thing I'll ever think. I'm petting my uncle, a cat and he's adorable. That sounds so fucking wrong.

Much to my amusement Gigi magics a collar out of thin air. When Lucifer is well and truly asleep, I attach the pink collar to him. When a fizzle and a flash of purple light flashes, I realise even more shockingly that it magically sealed so the idiot wouldn't be able to take it off.

Dad lays against the headboard beside me, with my mum laying against him. Gigi and Papi lay the other side of me. Jill lays along the bottom of the bed.

As everyone is drawn into the movie, I look around. How did I get so lucky to have so many people who love me?

Despite everything we've been through, we are stronger and bigger than ever. Now that my supernatural side has come out, I'll never have to leave the town again.

A knock sounds at the door. It opens revealing Xander. I smile at him, and he returns the gesture.

I pat the bed and he comes to join us. My Papi moves over slightly so Xander can cuddle into my side. I'm not even mad about him being close to me. For a woman who hates contact so much, I love contact with him.

I've no idea what to do about him falling asleep almost instantly, with his head resting on my chest. But I do know that I like it more than I should. I'm falling for the supernatural king.

Scrap that, I've already fallen. I think I'm in love with this man.

It's not long after that, I drift off into a peaceful sleep, surrounded by those who mean everything to me.

CHAPTER 24

"**A**im for the head," Hades orders me.

Doing as I'm told; I strike the mace into the mannequin's skull. The reinforced mannequins head shatters, much to everyone's surprise.

"They certainly weren't kidding when they said you're a berserker," Harriet offers, whistling at my strike.

Yeah, turns out berserkers weren't just Norse mythology. Apparently, they weren't even humans that went into a violent rage. They're more of the supernatural variety, that are literally built to fight. We also have a liking for blood, which is ironic considering they were called bloodthirsty. Or maybe that's the reason they're called bloodthirsty.

It was agreed I needed to train again, especially to learn the most effective ways of destroying wraiths, since they don't quite work the same way as other supernaturals.

"Right, so head shots are always a good shot to take," Hades explains. Of course they're a good shot to take. If something has no head or brain, they can't function. "It's not always the easiest shot to take, however. You're smaller than some which…"

I cut him off, "Can be a disadvantage. But I'm also highly skilled, unlike most of the people you typically train." I'm pretty sure Hades and Harriet keep forgetting that I may be new to the supernatural world, but I'm not new to violence and aggression.

"Sorry, I keep forgetting," Hades offers sheepishly. "I just keep seeing you flying into a tree and your back snapping like a twig," he remarks.

"If only I knew supernaturals were a thing. If only I knew I needed to carry an actual weapon, rather than dealing with problems with my fists," I offer sarcastically.

Harriet changes the training to something that's actually new. "You need to learn to shift," she states, and I frown. I didn't realise I was meant to shift. Typically, that's reserved for actual shifters. Like the sort that turn from human to animal. "You don't necessarily have another form, but in your berserker form your senses become even more heightened. Your movements swift and stealthy. Just because you have your strength and speed in this form it doesn't mean that by accessing the other side of you, you won't be even better."

So I'm not shifting? I'm so confused.

"How did you feel when you accessed your other form when in the command centre?" Hades asks.

Word has gotten around about that. Despite it being three days ago they're still talking about it as though it was yesterday. It would seem my tantrum has cost the King millions because of how much high-tech equipment was in that room. I destroyed it all. I should be sorry, but I'm really not. It was amazing. Even more so when I managed to destroy a couple of the walls of the room as well. They had been reinforced, but I managed to break right through them without any effort.

Thankfully no one expects me to pay for the replacement.

But in the three days since that incident, me and my family have forgiven one another and are back to normal. In fact, we are better than ever. I've also healed fully. Which is why I'm in this tragic excuse of a training session.

"I was angry," I answer Hades. I'd have thought that would be completely obvious.

"Just angry. So, if I was to goad you, maybe push you around a bit, your other side would appear?" he asks, and I see what he's saying.

"No," I offer, knowing it to be true. "I was furious. I wanted to rip everyone apart until there was nothing left," I explain, remaining rather calm.

"So, draw that feeling into yourself. Try to bring that rage back up," he offers, and I have to say that this is the absolute worst idea I have ever heard.

It's beyond stupid. I'm not the sort of person who can just switch off when I'm that enraged, and I will undoubtedly cause a fair bit of destruction.

"Don't do that," my Papi offers, butting into this training session. Turns out, just like me, he too is a berserker. "You need to be able to draw up your abilities when you need them, but you need to be able to maintain control. If you allow your anger to fuel you, then you won't maintain control," he explains.

"Huh, I didn't know that," Hades offers, not

even offering an apology for the shitty advice.

Choosing instead to ignore the lot of them, I try to scrounge up what the fiction books would suggest. I know they aren't true, but they're based on something. Maybe there is some logic in it all.

Some of the fantasy books would suggest emotion is the key to anything. Others also suggest emotion. I'm aware I said emotion twice. A lot of them just love being so overemotional. The ones that always resonated with me, however, are the ones that suggested imagining what you want to happen. By picturing it you allow your body to follow along.

Closing my eyes, I remember how it felt to be in my other form. Not the part where I was uncontrollably angry, but the parts where I felt so strong, I could crush stone. See so clearly, my vision was trained on my target, but my senses where so sharp that nothing could sneak up on me.

A tingle rushes through my body and fire starts to burn within me. Unlike last time it doesn't feel uncontrollable.

I hear gasps, and I open my eyes. The acute focus I have is amazing.

"Silver," Harriet and Hades say in unison. Obviously referring to my eye colour.

I've heard this a lot. Whenever my berserker comes out, my eyes change from blue to silver. Other than that, there aren't any physical changes, other than my fangs. They were a surprise, but at the same time it wasn't all that unexpected, given my habit of blood drinking.

"Well, she seems to know what she's doing," Harriet offers.

"She always does, when it comes to violence," Papi reveals. "Being organised, on time or completing homework was less her style," he adds, and I smile.

Hades and Harriet step back when they see me smile. My fangs are bigger than theirs, and I am apparently more of a predator than they are. There instincts tell them to fear me because the magic I give off overpowers them. It's similar to how most people react to my family. People back away, go silent, and on the rare occasion, they collapse under the fear. Yeah, I couldn't believe that was actually the case either, but I've actually seen people collapse because of them. It's rather amusing.

Knowing that I can bring my other side forth, I attempt to do the opposite and let it go. This time instead of thinking about my other form, I bring up the human side of me. The side that is softer and doesn't scare others into fleeing.

The side that is just as violent but isn't built for battle. I feel the magic fade, and when I open my eyes the surprise in those around me, suggest I was successful.

"I've never met someone who can so easily bring forth their other side," Hades gasps.

I know it's an odd situation when even my Papi is surprised.

"Neither have I," he exclaims. He's an immortal truth and I'm guessing he's been around for quite a while. The seriousness of his words makes me realise how big a deal it is that I have so much control for someone so new. "I expected you to bring your other side forth easily enough, but I didn't expect you to be able to let it go just as easily. How did you do it?"

"I just thought about what makes me human. How I'm softer and people don't flee from the power I give out. About the side that can fight, but isn't built for battle and it slipped away," I explain.

It occurs to me that I may be a bit of a freak, even in the supernatural world. It's not like I'm not used to it, as I was an outcast in the human world as well.

Something occurs to me, and I question how it took me so long to think of it.

"How many supernaturals did I hang around with as a child?" I ask my Papi.

"All but one of your acquaintances where powered," he answers.

"And supernaturals are automatically stronger than humans. Even witches?" I ask. He nods his head. "So how did a human take down so many supernaturals?" I ask. I was always getting into fights as a child, and there were only two times I didn't win.

"A human wouldn't. It's not possible," Papi explains.

It's Harriot who catches on to what I mean. "She means everyone thought she was human, which is why she was forced out. But she only hung around with supes, so how did she beat them?"

My Papi pauses and his face falls. "How did I not consider that? None of us did. But then why have your abilities taken so long to come forth? Nothing about you makes any sense," Papi grumbles. Then winces. "That wasn't meant as an insult in any way."

I brush him off. Since I've known my Papi my entire life, I know he didn't say anything as an insult. I can understand his confusion however. Why did it take so long for my abilities to come out? If I was supernatural, why did I react to the drug?

Having had enough of the conversation, I order my Papi to leave. I want to train with Hades and Harriot, rather than those I'm familiar with. Everyone has their own fighting style, and it gives me no end of intrigue, in learning other peoples. It often provides tips and tricks for things you'd never have thought about. Thankfully Papi leaves without complaint, and we get back to our fighting.

I start sparring with Hades, delighting in discovering how to fight supernaturals and actually being challenged in a fight for a change. Since Supernaturals have quicker reflexes, as well as heightened senses, it means I have to put more effort into the fight.

He swings and I duck. Swinging out myself and striking him in the gut. His other fist connects with my face, and I go flying from the impact. Jumping up, I rush at him. Instead of attacking, I swerve to the side at the last minute, and come up behind him. Kicking out, I strike his backside and send him crashing to the ground.

"Oh fuck," I hear someone grumble. It doesn't sound like Hades. "Watch it or I'll end up being swallowed whole, and I'm cosy enough where I am."

The voice distracts me enough for Hades to

get the upper hand. I'm not that bothered, since I'm more curious about who spoke.

"Who was that?" I ask the room.

"Who was what?" Harriot asks, from her spot watching me and Hade's spar. "You got distracted. I didn't think I'd have to tell you to focus on a fight."

"Who spoke? When I kicked Hades someone said, 'oh fuck,' then started talking about how cosy they were...," I taper off as I get a sneaking suspicion I know what happened. "Whoever spoke, what is your name?" I ask.

"She can hear me. This is amazing," the voice offers with a squeal. "I'm Abaddon the destroyer," it says, and I burst out laughing.

"Abaddon the Destroyer?" I marvel. Hades' cheeks go a deep crimson and I know I was right. He's got a butt plug in. Fuck, as much as that power is annoying as hell, it seems it also allows for some amusing situations, and I might be starting to enjoy it.

"Who's Abaddon the destroyer? Isn't that a devil?" Harriot asks. Now that I know that Lucifer is real, I get the feeling Abaddon is as well.

"How do you know?" Hades asks seriously.

"Yeah, so the girls may have neglected to mention to avoid magical spells and potions after the ceremony, and as a result I took a libido enhancement potion. Instead of increased libido, I got the biggest cock block of all time. I can speak to sex toys!" I explain.

Instead of getting angry about it, he bursts out laughing until tears roll down his cheeks.

"Hades are you wearing a butt plug called Abaddon the destroyer?" Harriot asks. "Why did you name it Abaddon?"

"Why do you think I called it Abaddon the Destroyer. It's not exactly small and timid," he offers and it's my turn to laugh.

"I love it when he laughs. It feels like he's choking me," the voice, sorry, Abaddon the Destroyer, offers. I laugh so hard I end up wheezing.

I relay the message to the others, and we end the session by breaking down into helpless fits of giggles, like we are schoolkids laughing over a dirty word.

CHAPTER 25

After the eventful training session with Hades and Harriot, they took me up to the newly renovated command centre.

Everyone agreed that it would be in everyone's best interest for me to be involved in solving this problem, especially since it's me who's being attacked constantly. Despite all my temper issues, I've got a good rap sheet when it comes to defending others, and with the knowledge that I can withstand a wraiths toxin, it's a smart move. They can use me as bait, knowing that I am more than capable of defending myself.

"Hello," a middle-aged man offers, with a nod of acknowledgement. He holds his hand out, and I place mine in his for a firm handshake. "You must be Freyja Heathen, it's a pleasure to meet you. I'm Griffin, the Supernatural Guard Force Captain," he explains.

The oh so helpful Hades, murmurs in my ear that the Captain is the man in charge. Just below the King of course. Despite Griffins obvious power level, I'm not intimidated one bit. Again, I suspect that is more telling about the sheer level of power within me.

The captain leaves me, Hades and Harriot to go collect some information from those around the room. Alexis and her brother, Dane, are there, along with Jill. I still feel anger towards Dane, but it's not even close to the levels it used to be. I suspect it will take some time to get over the fact that he wasn't doing anything to harm me and was simply doing as he was told. But years of conditioning, telling me he is the problem, will be hard to break.

I'm surprised how quickly they managed to get the command centre up and running again. It still has monitors covering all walls and has a table in the centre of the room, but they also have one large monitor on the far wall, that can display whatever is needed. It's pretty much the same as before, only the equipment is new, since almost every single item in here was trashed by me.

"Gather around," Griffins states, and people follow his orders.

Hades practically drags me to the table because I didn't move at the order. I had no idea if it was for me or not. Obviously, I was told that I'd be included, but didn't figure I'd be in the inner circle.

"All the intel gathered, tells us the threat is a group who call themselves 'The Darkness'," Griffin explains. "This isn't necessarily a terrorist group, however. Everything points towards them being intent on one goal and that is destroying Freyja," he explains, and all eyes turn to me.

"Naughty. Naughty. What did you do?" Hades jokes.

Slapping the back of his head, I focus on the captain. "Why do they want to kill me?"

"I was hoping you could tell me," he reveals.

"Hell if I know," I remark. "We'd spoke about this before," I start not saying anything about the time I trashed the room. "I was asked who has a problem with me, and honestly the list is too long to count," I offer. Dane and Jill snort out a laugh, and I have to admit it's pretty funny.

Since I know both of them from when I was a child, and was close with both of them, they saw all the fights I got into. They know that I speak the truth.

"While that may be true, it will most likely

be someone who you've either met since moving here, or someone who knows you were moving home," Dane says, and I can't help wincing at his choice of words. Moving home after being booted out.

"Well that certainly shortens the list. Karen obviously hates me, although I have no idea what happened to her. My ex knows I moved back here, but he's human," I explain. Other than that, I can't think of anyone else who would have it out for me.

"Are you sure your ex is human?" a lady besides Griffin asks. Judging by how close she is to him; I'd hazard a guess that they're family.

"I'd say yes because he hated anything rooted in fantasy, but honestly I don't know. I doubt I'd have known it unless I saw it," I explain.

"If he was supernatural, he wouldn't just marry anyone. Someone that young would still be waiting for their mate," Alexis explains.

Everyone nods, but I get caught up on that word again.

"What's a mate?" I ask, realising I never did ask before. Gigi had called Xander my mate, but I didn't know what it meant. I'd assumed it was a term for a friend, but it doesn't seem that is the way they are using it. After everything that happened that day, it had slipped my mind.

Judging by the way people talk about mates, I believe it's something they revere and love.

"A mate is what a human may call a soulmate. It's someone you are destined to be with. There's an instant connection, and that's because you were made for one another," the woman besides Griffin says, adoration shining in her eyes when she looks to the captain. Ah, so they're mates.

Shit. The blood drains from my face as I realise what that means. Could Gigi be telling the truth? Is Xander my mate? Is that why, despite the fact I want to beat him on a good day, I also feel so completely attracted to him?

"Oh," is all I can muster.

"Have you heard someone say that you're their mate?" Jill asks, knowing shines in her eyes.

"Certainly not my ex-husband," I respond instead. Under no circumstances will I reveal the possibility of their King being my soulmate.

"Well Karen was released," Griffins explains, oblivious to the tension in the air. "She was banished from the town for her behaviour and ordered not to step foot in here again. She also has a spell on her that ensures she isn't able to enter the grounds."

"She's a banshee, so doesn't have the

right magic to raise wraiths. But she does have connections, so could be the one truly responsible," Griffin's mate explains.

"But we don't know anything for certain," I remark. Truthfully, I'm just saying what everyone else is thinking. We all know there's no proof it's Karen. We all know that we don't have any leads, other than they're attacking me. "So how are we going to get more information into the matter?" I ask, suspecting I know the answer.

"Honestly, other than using you as bait, there isn't much choice. Even then we'd need to have the capable people following you 24 hours a day, so if you were attacked, they'd be able to attempt to track the magic," Griffins explains.

"But," Alexis emphasises glaring at Griffins in annoyance, "Freyja hasn't completely transitioned. Meaning despite it still being difficult to kill you, it's still possible."

I understand her concern, but I can be attacked at any point. I've already been attacked three times, and only once was I in a position where I had actual back up, and I died that day. At least in this situation, I'd have back up if I needed it.

If they can track the magical signature being used, it could provide an important lead, that we can use to end this once and for all.

"How do you permanently stop wraiths?" I ask. It's possible I've already been told but I still need to check.

"You have to kill the one who is controlling them," Jill explains.

"So, we need to know who's raising them. To do that we need to track the magic being used. To do that we need bait. Also known as me. After all, it's me they're attacking," I explain to Alexis. I agree with Griffin's plan. When Alexis goes to argue, I state, "Whether I'm used as bait or not, I have a good chance of being attacked. At least this way, I have support if I need it. I haven't during the past occurrences."

"I've seen her fight sis," Dane pipes in. "She's a force to be reckoned with, and if she is comfortable with it, I'll stick to her to provide the backup she might need. I've helped her before," he offers.

Despite still having some reluctance with him, I have to admit we made a good team. We had one another's backs and he's incredibly skilled.

"Fine," Alexis relents. "But you have to protect her. I understand you are strong Freyja, but you're still new to this world, and I don't want to lose you when I've only just met you. You're a firecracker that has to be around for a long, long time," she explains.

I love how protective she's getting over me. I've got to admit I've become very fond of her, Rosemary and Elana over the short time we've known each other.

"Plus, it's not everyday someone gets all hot and bothered over a vampire bite at the ceremony spell. I need to know what else is odd about you," she offers with a sneaky grin.

"Is that why the King was grinning so much?" Griffins Mate asks with round eyes.

"Wait," Jill screeches with excitement lacing her words. "Is he your mate?"

Silence descends the room as all eyes turn to me. Clearly, they're wanting a response, and all of them are invested in it.

"I hope you are. He needs to find his mate soon before the curse gets him," Hades states seriously.

"There is no curse on my family," a new voice calls. Turning, I find a man who looks similar to Xander, only a little more mature. "Reginald was mad to begin with," he adds. I've no idea who Reginald is, but my guess is he lost his mind in some way.

"What?" I ask. "Didn't you mention something about that at the cemetery?" I ask

Hades and Harriot. "I'm sure you did, because then you said that the councilman would have your guts for garters if he heard you say it."

A boisterous laugh rings through the room from the new guy, "Yea, I do have a habit of ripping peoples guts out," he offers, and already I like him more. His expression turns serious all of a sudden, and that pointed glare turns my way. "Although, I suggest that you learn some respect to your King young lady."

Ah, got to love it when people complain about me calling the king, Xander. I'm not in the habit of using titles with people I believe are equals. Xander has treated me as an equal, and has never voiced an issue with the informality. I'm not going to let this guy rip into me.

"I'll give him some respect, when he stops pissing me the hell off," I remark calmly.

Anger turns his expression, and if I was to guess, I'd say he's two seconds away from trying to rip me apart. My change comes over me with ease, and his eyes widen but he doesn't back down.

"Is the King your mate?" Jill almost screams at me.

"Yes," I scream back at her, while my gaze remains on the newcomer.

With my words ringing like a gunshot in the air, the man calms down instantly. Calmness descends, and without the hostile power in the air, I allow my own abilities to fade back.

"You're my son's mate?" the man asks. Shit, it's his father. No wonder he was so concerned about my lack of respect.

"According to my grandmother," I remark.

"Who's your grandmother?" he asks.

"Mother Nature," Jill responds.

"Oh, thank fuck for that. He's not going to lose his mind," Xander's father states.

Clearly even he believes in this supposed curse. It's probably bullshit, and it's likely more to do with ruling an entire area for so long without someone's support. Without having someone you can trust by your side.

I've been here for less than a month. I've been attacked three times. Had a run-in with a bitch who nearly drove into me. I've met far too many people who will likely become a big part of my life. Now I've got to act as bait to catch some idiots trying to kill me. Now I've learnt I have a mate, who is also known as a soulmate. I don't know how to be a good wife, as should be evident by the divorce. I wanted a peaceful familiar place to find myself and call home. Instead, it's been one set of dramas after another.

I'm so done with the supernatural world.

CHAPTER 26

I walk down the hallway towards my room in the estate. Turns out I have a room on the 4th floor. When I woke up in a room after my accident, it was actually Xander's room. I suppose there were numerous signs he and I were meant to be, but I just didn't realise it at the time.

Jill had explained that for the few days I was unconscious, Xander had been difficult to find. We now know it's because he was watching over me and trying to help as much as he was able to.

I don't know how I'm meant to feel about everything. Obviously, I wasn't planning on finding someone so soon after the messy as hell divorce, but if this mate thing is true, then how can I deny it. Even I can admit I find myself more drawn to Xander then I have been with anyone else before.

But then again, do I really want to start something when there is already so much going on. I'm under threat at the moment by an unknown group. I'm still trying to learn about this new world I've been thrown into. I've also got a ridiculous amount of family to meet.

Although maybe having a constant will be good. My feelings for him grow every day, and alright those feelings usually include annoyance, but honestly, I'm not one for lovey dovey shit. My language of love is sarcasm, and he can handle that. After all, he's just as bad as I am in that sense.

"Hey Freyja, can we talk?" Xander asks, jogging to catch up to me. Speak of the devil and he shall appear. Or in this case, think of him and he shall appear.

"Sure. What's up?" I ask.

"There's something I need to tell you," he says, nerves have him fidgeting.

"That we're mates?" I ask, hoping to ease his anxiety a bit.

"You know?" he asks.

"Yeah. We were just talking about it. Obviously, this was after your father tried to fight me for calling you Xander, rather than the king," I offer.

"You met my father?" he asks. "I bet that was entertaining," he adds with a chuckle.

"It sure was," I answer. "Could you explain to me a bit more about us being mates. I understand it's similar to a soulmate but how do you know we are mates? What does it really mean?" I ask.

He directs me towards my room, and we head inside. He takes a seat in the armchair, while I sit on my very comfortable bed.

"Mates are those who were born for one another. Some see it as taking the choice out of someone's hands, but I see it more as knowing there is someone out there who is a perfect fit. Someone who will accept me for me. They're highly prized because they are difficult to find," he starts explaining, and it says a lot that I didn't feel like the choice was taken from me. Despite our spats, even I can admit I get along with him brilliantly, and I do have a fascination with him. "When you meet them there is an instant connection. You feel like your heart is truly beating for the first time in your life," he explains. I can tell he's struggling to put into words what he felt. But I know what he means.

"I know what you mean," I explain. "What else is involved with being mates?" I ask, getting the impression that just like my transition, our mate bond, isn't complete.

"When we first sleep together we will bite one another," he explains, and a shiver races through me at the thought. "It solidifies the bond between us, and we will gain a sense of where one another are, as well as how we are feeling. It's all part of the connection," he explains.

Despite having reservations before, I can't deny that I want this more than I've wanted anything in my life.

For the first time in my life, I decide to listen to what my heart is telling me. I should just go for it. After all, mates aren't a common occurrence, and I believe him when he says that. Everyone seems to hold mate bonds as something truly wonderful, and I can imagine why if it already feels this amazing just being around him.

Getting up, I waltz over to Xander. Straddling his lap, I go in for a kiss, which he returns. It starts sweet but quickly turns to animal passion. I'm lifted into his arms, and he walks us over to the bed.

With me welcoming the bond, my body goes into hyperdrive, and I crave Xander's touch. With that one kiss, I've become addicted to him, and I doubt I'd be able to let him go even if I tried. My hands glide into his hair and I hold him to me, not wanting to ever let him go.

Our clothes quickly vanish in between kissing, until we are both naked and eager to complete our mating bond.

"Are you sure?" Xander asks, staring me deep in my eyes.

I'm guessing it takes a lot for him to ask since he is more than ready.

"Absolutely," I say, truthfully. I really do mean it. With the acknowledgement that it's the mating bond I've been feeling with him, I no longer feel the need to deny myself.

He thrusts into me and it's like my whole world crumbles and reforms brighter and better than ever. I've definitely made the right decision. As my orgasm builds, I get the intense urge to bite his neck. I don't fight it. My teeth sink into the soft flesh on his neck, and I hold onto him for dear life, allowing his warm blood to pool in my mouth. He does the same, and his teeth pierce my skin. Bliss envelops me, and I release him to scream out my orgasm. He's quick to follow, and we are left panting in the wake of what is likely to be the best orgasm I've ever had.

We lay for some time in bed. Cuddling close to one another as we work to catch our breath and pull ourselves back together.

"What will change?" I ask him seriously. Things like this always lead to change of some kind, but I have no idea what. After the failed marriage I've no idea what to expect and I don't have much good experience to go on.

"You'll become mine and everyone else's Queen," he says.

I laugh. When he doesn't join in, I look to his face. He raises an eyebrow and I realise he's being serious. Fuck! He's the King and we are essentially together forever now, which would make me a Queen. Will people even accept me as a Queen? I'll make a terrible ruler. I'm far too violent.

What does it mean to be a queen? Am I expected to act like a lady, because that is truly never going to happen. If he expects that of me, I will rip him a new arsehole and I'll borrow Melvin to do it. Or maybe I'll ask Hades if I can borrow Abaddon the destroyer for a bit.

"Stop fretting," Xander orders, and I scowl at him. How could he tell I was worrying? "Supernaturals are inherently a violent race. Obviously, some are more so than others, but no one is going to expect you to be regal, calm and polite. We all know that would be expecting too much of you," he jokes, and I slap him.

"They won't accept me," I state. I'm sure of it. "I'm a species known to thrive in wars and battles. I've no idea how to be a Queen and I'm sure they'd all prefer someone more... sociable," I add.

Growing up, I'd always wanted to do something physical. Boxing, or wrestling, or martial arts. I'd looked into careers for those specific qualities, and I'd found security work or championships. Since I'm not one for the spotlight, security work was my dream job. It was always considered an odd job to be my dream job, but it allowed me to do the one thing I love above all else.

My backup job option was teaching. Again that sounds extremely weird coming from someone who struggles with patience, but I love kids. I'm so incredibly protective of them, and I'd like to think I'd be good at providing children with the skills they need to be successful.

But never, in my entire life, did I expect to be a queen. That's not something I ever wanted. Even as a young girl, I'd never gone around saying I was a princess. If anything, I said I was a soldier. If I thought discovering the supernatural would be the biggest surprise, I was seriously wrong.

"I think you'll be surprised at how readily they accept you," he offers, kissing me on the head. I enjoy feeling small and protected in his arms. I may love fighting more than anything else, but even I can admit how nice it is to feel secure and safe. "You are my mate. You were born for this even if you don't realise it just yet," he offers.

I leave the conversation there, not wanting to dwell on the future when I have a battle coming up.

"Is there anything else I need to know?" I ask my mate.

He thinks for a moment before saying, "Nothing of urgency. Obviously, I would love for you to move to the estate on a more permanent basis. But if accommodation is a sticking point, we can compromise. I'll have to ask Rosemary and Elana if they can pull together helpers to get your crowning ceremony planned. But for now, my Jailbird, don't worry about anything. I'll sort everything out, and you can shout to your hearts content about it later," he offers, giving me a broad grin.

Well at least he's not under the impression I'll be a quiet submissive partner. It seems he knows me better than I expected.

Knocking on the door has the pair of us groaning in annoyance. Xander stands up and wraps himself in a dressing gown, before plodding over to open the door.

"Hey, your most royal majesty," Jill greets sarcastically.

Something tells me, with the knowledge me and Xander are mates, she's treating him like a normal sibling or family member, as opposed to a member of the royal family. She pokes her head into the room, and spots me laid in bed with only a sheet covering my naked body. Her eyes go wide when she sees me.

"Holy shit, you guys already mated?" she asks in disbelief.

"Why are you here?" I ask her.

"Well, I came to tell him that Jack's in town," she explains. Then clarifies, "your ex-husband."

"He's what?" I shout. "Why would you be telling him that, instead of me?" I ask in annoyance.

"Because I was hoping he'd get rid of your ex before you found out. I'm expecting lots of violence otherwise, and with your newfound supernatural strength that's a recipe for a murder charge," she explains.

Score one to Jill. Even I can understand her reasoning.

"How did you know Xander was here?" I ask. We're in the room I was assigned. Xander's room is on the 6th floor of the building.

"People said they saw him with you and

mentioned you headed into a room. I'd expected you to be making out at most. But you guys mated! Urgh, I can't wait to be an auntie," she squeals in delight. I choke at the thought of having kids. Xander grins and I suspect he'd like to have children. That will have to be a conversation for another day.

"What does the dickhead want?" I ask Jill, referring to my ex in my favourite name for him.

"He's going around town asking for your whereabouts. It seems he's desperate to talk to you," Jill adds.

Groaning, I flop back in bed. Just when I was starting to be happy, he has to show up and ruin it all. If I don't talk to him, he'll never leave, so I'm going to have to hunt him down. The sooner I talk to him, the quicker he will piss off.

Let the shit show commence.

CHAPTER 27

Despite being rather insistent, I refuse to let Xander come with me to deal with my ex. He's being protective and understands I can't stand the man, but I don't need to poke the bear. Plus, if anyone is going to beat the living snot out of the dickhead, it'll be me.

So now I'm on my way to Sue's bakery to meet up with my dickhead ex-husband. I'm actually rather curious about what he could possibly want, since we'd both been rather adamant neither of us wanted to see each other again.

Opening the doors to the bakery, I stroll over to the counter. Sue sees me and flags me over. She's currently got a queue of about twenty to get through, so I head behind the counter and help her get through them. Since I'm early to the meeting with my ex I know I have time to kill, especially since he's known to show up late.

When the queue has finally been cleared, Sue turns to me with a quirked brow.

"Dare I ask what brings you here?" she states.

"I get the feeling you already know," I remark. Nothing happens in this town that she isn't aware about. After all the bakery is the centre of the town and gossip runs rampant here. Not only that but Sue seems to be the unofficial towns messenger. Everyone tells her all the news and just like a sponge she soaks it all up. Everyone knows that the necessary people will be informed of any situations and that Sue won't spread rumours. Everyone trusts her and turns to her for guidance. It's another reason I was so surprised she'd managed to run the bakery by herself.

"That I do. Your ex-husband is in town," she remarks.

"That he is. I figured I might as well meet the prick here rather than anywhere else," I explain. "After all, this place has pastries and mama loves her sugar," I chuckle.

"Grab whatever you want but make the prick pay," she states.

Since the secret is out about my

supernatural side, I grab a pastry from the sanguine range. Thankfully this time I shouldn't get a deep wrenching hunger, since I've already had some blood today. Despite her telling me to help myself, I head over to the register and put the money in for my pastries when she isn't looking. She's super kind and generous, but I don't want to be responsible for her losing money.

I've only just sat down, when the shit stain comes strolling in like he owns the place. Looking to the clock for the time, I see its ten minutes past the hour. He's ten minutes late, as expected.

Jack heads over to the counter and clicks his fingers to get Sue's attention. The look she gives him is a promise of violence.

"You're not from around here so let me explain. The next time you click your fingers at me I will break them and nobody, not the police or patrons, will punish me for it," she warns.

I whistle in surprise. I've never seen her so serious and deadly. She means it as well. I know without a shadow of a doubt, that she means it.

Clearly Jack isn't as stupid as he looks. After grabbing a pastry and coffee, he searches the room until he spots me. Strutting over, he gives me the charming smile I once loved. Now it has my blood boiling in my veins, and I'm desperate to strike a punch. Or maybe a smash with the maces,

I do in fact have on my person.

"Good afternoon, Freyja," he offers, with that charming smile still plastered to his fake arse face.

"What do you want? I have shit to do," I say seriously.

"What could you possibly need to do in this ...," he pauses, looking around the room in disgust, "backwards little town."

I just quirk my brow at him, waiting for him to answer my question.

"You need to come home," he states. I continue glaring at him. "You're my wife. You need to stop with this temper tantrum and come home."

I can't believe he'd actually say that. Even after being with him all that time, I didn't expect him to say that. Obviously, I divorced him, but that doesn't change the fact that without me in his life he could find someone else who maybe doesn't respect themselves enough to be with a decent human being. Maybe someone who's fine being treated as a piece of property. I'm not sure there is anyone out there like that, but miracles can happen.

"Ex-wife," I state. "We are no longer married Jack. We got divorced. This 'backward little town' is my home. Now what is the real reason you're here?" I ask knowing that there has to be a more substantial reason. After all he spent more time arguing with me, than happy with me. He hated that marriage as much as I did. Although, he probably hated it because I refused to be at his beck and call. He wanted a housewife; I wanted a life that I could leave.

"He probably wants a wife to show off to his colleagues and family, while he's taking it up the ass by that whore," I hear someone say, and the coffee I had just taken a sip of comes flying from my nose.

"What the hell is wrong with you? You were always so disgusting and unladylike," Jack scoffs, wiping his hand down his face where some of the coffee landed on him.

I've gotten a little more used to hearing random voices, since it's surprising how many people have sex toys on their persons. But I did not expect to ever hear one coming from Jack. He's one of the most homophobic people I've met.

"I don't know. I've heard you like a woman who can top your bottom," I remark. For the briefest of moments, he is surprised. But he quickly covers it up with a scowl.

But for that one second, his perfect façade slipped and that's all I need to know. Who would've thought. That one little slip confirms that he is in fact, the one with a sex toy on his person.

"You're just disgusting," he growls.

"You always did have a stick up your arse," I fire back. Then I smile and add, "Or maybe it's more like a plug."

He brushes off what I say. Moving to stare out of the window.

"You need to come home. Not stay here in this supernatural spooktacular shithole of a town," he states.

It's my turn to frown. He's never mentioned anything about the supernatural before, or at least not in a way that suggests he believes in it. It's possible he's only saying it because of the ghost stories as well as the myths and legends of the town, but I'm getting the impression that's not what he is referring to.

"Since when have you been open to the supernatural?" I ask, eyeing Sue who keeps watch on the situation.

My guess is she's also listening in. Now that I look, I see multiple people, including my neighbours Maggie and Jon, watching the exchange closely. Score one for the Supernatural spooktacular shithole. This community watches out for each other.

"It's a figure of speech you freak," he growls.

"Yeah, say that to the witch who rams you every night. Honestly, I'm surprised I've not gotten lost yet. Gaped and flappy, that's what you are," that unknown voice says again. I again snort out a laugh at that. I really don't care if people think I'm crazy. The amount you can learn from sex toys is very surprising.

"Yeah? Is that so?" I question, referring to his supposed use of figure of speech.

I eye him cautiously, watching for any tells he has. When he can't look me in the eye, I realise that what the butt plug said is true. He knows that supernaturals exist and apparently, he is in fact fucking a witch.

Is it possible Jack knows about me? Why does he suddenly want me to come back, when he was just as insistent on the divorce as I was? What game is he playing? I know he's playing a game, but I also know he's not going to tell me outright what he's playing at.

"You are coming home," Jack orders, and I roll my eyes.

"Sorry but I've got maces to smash into skulls, and creatures of the night to kill," I remark, and again I watch for his tells.

He scratches his head and looks away from me. "You're a psycho," he states, standing up. "If you're not going to come willingly, I'll be back and it will be something you can't refuse," he warns.

Ah shit, is he going to get me locked in a psychiatric facility again?

He did that once. Claimed I'd lost my mind, all because I didn't want to give him £10,000 of my well-earned money, all so he could start up another failed business. I was pissed, especially because he had money of his own but demanded mine.

Since, despite him being a dick, he does have connections, he managed to get a doctor's signature stating I was a danger to myself and others. I spent two weeks in a psychiatric facility run by others that Jack knew. I only managed to get out after I'd stolen a phone and contacted my boss, who wasn't a complete arsehole. He'd got in touch with the right people, and I'd been allowed to leave, after they confirmed there wasn't actually anything wrong. Technically they said I had anger issues, but they also agreed that I could control them well enough to be deemed safe for society. It's after that, I worked on getting a divorce.

With that thought in mind, I glare at the jackass in front of me. All the while my mind runs through possibilities of what he could do to make things difficult for me.

When he realises, I won't change my mind with his threat, he stands up abruptly, knocking his chair over in the process, before storming from the bakery. The dick doesn't even bother picking his chair up.

Those listening into the conversation, turn to me expectantly. Sue comes over with another pastry that she places in front of me, before she takes a seat in the spot Jack just vacated.

"I feel there was some of that conversation we didn't hear. Do you want to tell us?" Sue asks.

I debate if I want to talk so openly with those in the café, but honestly, it's not a secret that wraiths have been attacking. It's just a secret that they seem to be aiming to destroy me.

"He had, what I think was a butt plug in, that was rather chatty," I explain.

"Who knew talking to sex toys would be so helpful," Sue laughs.

"It mentioned Jack has been taking it in the ass by a witch. It could be a figure of speech, but when I mentioned the creatures of the night, he couldn't look me in the eye. He also scratched his head. He knows more than he's letting on, and somehow, I think he's partially responsible for the wraiths," I explain being truthful. As soon as he mentioned the town being supernatural, I knew something was up.

The question now is why is he so desperate to have me back home, when I'm almost certain he's trying to kill me?

"He had a mind block in place," Maggie offers.

Turning to her, I frown. A mind block?

"A human can't block their thoughts from telepaths, without magical intervention," Maggie explains.

Makes sense. But who is the witch?

So, who are involved other than Jack? Why are they so desperate to kill me? What could I have possibly done to these people, to earn a death sentence?

CHAPTER 28

Me, Jill, Alexis, Rosemary and Elana all sit around the living room of Xander's rooms. I chucked him out so that we could have a girl's night. He willingly went, which is for the best. He wouldn't have won that battle.

"He was wearing a butt plug?" Alexis asks, cackling loudly.

I'd told them about my encounter with my ex-husband yesterday, and the ladies being the wicked women they are, found it endlessly amusing.

"It reminds me of the time that kid bought his mums anal beads into school, and called them a rocket," Jillian adds, and the reminder has me howling.

It's true. At the time none of us knew what

he had actually bought in, but for the kids 18th birthday it was bought up, and we all realised what it actually was. It was fantastic and so funny.

"I don't know if it was a butt plug or something else. What I do know is that he had some sort of sex toy on his person, and it was that, that told me about him being with some witch," I explain.

"Well, I'd imagine it's a dark witch...," Rose falters in her words looking to Elana with a heartbroken expression.

"What's wrong?" I ask, sensing there is some history there.

Rose looks to Elana, clearly stating that it's Elana's place to divulge that information, if she wishes. Judging by the way Elana clenches her jaw, it's not a good story.

Despite the conversations we've had in the past, I've never asked about family. Rosemary has a small family with just her mother and brother. Jillian obviously has Mark and Eve, her parents. I've met Alexis' brother and mother, although I have no idea if she has anyone else. But Elana is surprisingly quiet and doesn't often talk too much about herself. Usually any talking she does is about others rather than herself. There must be some history there.

"My parents turned dark," Elana states softly. "Rose is right though. To raise the dead means they're using black magic. Don't get me wrong dark magic isn't always bad, but those with it, have the power to do such a thing," she explains.

It's clear she doesn't want to talk too much about it, which is understandable. But at the same time, I really want to know what happened to her parents.

"What happened to them?" I ask softly. If she doesn't want to answer, I'll respect that, but there's no harm in asking.

"They got into a fight with a child," she starts, and already I'm shocked. "They were arrested for it, and the police found evidence of using dark magic for heinous crimes. They were sent to prison, and I've never seen them since. Some supernatural prisons don't allow visitation," she explains.

"Oh Elana, I'm so sorry," I say.

That must have been so difficult to go through. Especially for her, who's now lost her parents. Although it's likely for the best if her parents were using magic for criminal activity.

Jill looks around the room clearly sensing the tension evident in the air.

"So clearly the witch responsible is powerful. The question is, what powerful witch would want revenge on you," Jill asks, moving the topic on.

"Did you and your brother access my school records?" I ask Alexis. That was the reason Dane had even entered the room the day of my tantrum.

"Yeah. I've actually got a list of people in the school at the time you attended," she explains. Heading over to her bag, she pulls out a wad of papers and dumps them on the coffee table.

Despite the fact this day was meant to be for laughing and joking. Maybe enjoying some casual gossip, it seems to have moved to an investigation. That's fine with me because the sooner this is sorted, the sooner I can move on with my life.

Picking the papers up, I read through the list. Then, deciding to at least sort through them a bit, I acquire a couple of highlighters. As I go through the list, I highlight those I know. It's not as many as you'd expect. I also highlight the names of those I was good friends with at the time.

As I do this, the girls chat amongst themselves about the situation.

"Sorry girls, I have to go," Elana interrupts.

She's cheered up a bit since earlier, which I'm happy about. "I'll see you later," she offers.

As Elana leaves, we carry on trying to figure this mystery out. Once I've gone through the list, I lay the papers out on the table. There are only about 25 names highlighted. Turns out I only needed to highlight four names for who I knew well, Dane, Jill, Harriot and Missy. I've not spoken to Harriot and Missy since I left, and honestly, we weren't super close, but they were still good friends.

"Is there anyone on the highlighted list, who are powerful witches?" I ask the others.

They give the list a good look, sometimes offering the type of supernatural each person is. Once they're done with those I've highlighted, they move onto those who I haven't.

After some time, they sit up.

Rose says, "There's only two people on that list who have the power level capable of raising the dead. Tessa and Harry."

"I don't remember them," I explains.

"I do. I can't see it being either of them. I've spoken to them since Freyja left town and both didn't have a problem with her. They even said how sad and unexpected it was that she failed the test," Jill explains. Despite the mention of that goddamn test, I manage to stay calm.

"So, in other words, we've just spent the past two hours looking for clues and have yet to figure anything out," I grumble, getting irritated by this entire situation.

"Maybe not. I know Tessa's mum is also a powerful witch, and for the right price, she'll do just about anything. Maybe the witch responsible isn't someone with a problem with you, but is actually being paid for it," Rose explains. "It's quite a common business nowadays. Although for most, there isn't enough money in the world to create wraiths," she adds.

I mull over all the information. Something just isn't adding up. Jack is a prick, and I wouldn't put it past him to learn of the supernatural and to use that against me. But how did he learn about it all in the first place? I didn't even know about it, and I was raised with the supernatural.

Then there's this witch. Who is she? Was the butt plug, or whatever it was, on Jack's person, being figurative or literal, when it said Jack was sleeping with a witch? If it was being literal, then how did they meet? If figurative, then who is it, and how did they meet? How did they get a witch involved in all of this?

"My gut is telling me there is more than just Jack and the witch," I state.

"I was going to suggest the same thing," Rose explains. "Jack doesn't have magic. He's human. But the amount of wraiths that have been raised, is more than what just one witches power could raise. They'd need another magical being to gain enough magic. It doesn't have to be another witch. Any magical being can be used," she explains.

I'm glad these guys are my friends because they've been amazing helping me learn all about the supernatural world. If it weren't for their patience and caring, I wouldn't be as adjusted as I currently am. They don't care about having to explain the basics to me, and for that, I will be forever grateful.

"The first attack was the cemetery, and there was only the one wraith," Jill starts. "It's possible this witch and Jack assumed this would be enough to kill you. Afterall no one could know that you're not any ordinary supernatural. When that didn't work, they likely upped the attacks, hoping to use numbers to overwhelm and kill you," she explains.

There's one part of that explanation that I can't quite understand.

"What do you mean I'm not an ordinary supernatural?" I ask.

There's a moment where Jill goes wide

eyed, as though she's slipped up.

"She means you survived the wraith toxin. That's not an ordinary thing to survive, meaning you are most definitely not normal," Alexis offers.

I get the impression there's more to it than that, but I can't be bothered to get into that just yet.

There's a knock on the door and it opens. Xander pokes his head inside with a beaming smile on his face.

"Hey ladies, am I alright to come in?" he asks.

Since our girl's day turned into an investigation, I wave him inside. It would seem none of us can get this mystery from our mind.

"So, what have you been up to, my Jailbird?" Xander asks, and I smile. I've got to admit I love that nickname and it is accurate. Although I've never been in prison, I've spent many a day in Jail.

We fill Xander in on what we've been discussing, and he goes quiet as his mind gets to work.

"Well, I'd have thought it'd be obvious," he states. Us ladies, gawk at him. Did he just call us stupid. "I don't mean anything nasty by it. Afterall it's the first person you mentioned when we asked who you've pissed off," Xander offers.

I think on that. When I realise what he means, I smack my forehead.

"Karen!" I offer.

I think on it a little bit more and start forming a possible timeline of events.

"Alright, so Jack knew I was moving to my hometown. He knew where that was. I'm not entirely sure when he's met this witch, but I'd hazard that he did sometime between us divorcing and me moving," I offer. Everyone listens with rapt attention. "Then when I arrive, the witch raised a single wraith to kill me. It didn't work. So, they started looking for other people they could get to join them in destroying me," I explain.

"They found Karen who obviously hates you for beating her up and embarrassing her. She joins the crew, and the witch is able to raise even more wraiths with her help. They use sheer numbers to overwhelm but my brother ends up helping you," Alexis says.

"When you survived that, they blew up the car hoping that would weaken you enough to finally finish you off. Again, this would have worked, but you're incredibly protective of Xander and were fighting to defend him. Then your supernatural side kept you alive enough until you got back to the estate," Rose says.

"But who is the witch?" I scream, hating not knowing. "And since when does that homophobic prick of a man, take it up the arse?" I ask, no one in particular.

That's the hardest bit to understand. Jack hated me even being on top. He was one of those pricks who liked to believe he was a dominant man. Since I'm surprisingly bratty and submissive in bed, I didn't mind too much, but it still pisses me off that he's letting some bitch do it to him.

The others laugh at my outburst. I'm not surprised they laugh. If it was one of them whose ex is now willing to bottom when they wouldn't with them, I'd find it hilarious as well.

Another knock at the door has us all groaning. Since everyone we speak to is here, and my parents would message me and my grandparents would just let themselves in, it can only mean one of us is needed. When the knock sounds again, I get the impression it's urgent.

"It's open," I shout. I'm far too comfortable to get up.

The door opens and Hades enters.

"Sorry to bother you," he offers, smiling at me. "We've just received word that your house has been broken into Freyja," he says.

My house has been broken into. The place I grew up in. The place all my prized possessions are.

My heart rate picks up as my anger surfaces. It would seem my transition is nearly complete because I can sense my magic coiling inside me as my anger increases.

"Freyja, take a deep breath. We'll figure out who did it," Xander explains, as he stands up and backs away from me.

"They won't get away with it," I growl, and I don't even recognise my own voice.

The power inside me keeps growing and growing, until it bursts from me in a shower of light.

As the light fades, I'm stunned into silence.

Holy fucking shit!

CHAPTER 29

Despite me being stood in mine and Xander's rooms, at the estate, only moments ago, I'm now in the familiar surroundings of my childhood home. Somehow, I've managed to transport myself from the estate to my childhood home. No one mentioned that was something a berserker could do.

I'm in what was once my living room. But the sofa has been shredded, the table broken and a couple of boxes, I'd not managed to unpack, have been thrown across the room, smashing the contents to tiny pieces. Picture frames have been trashed with the images inside torn up.

Rushing to the kitchen, I find even more mess. My mugs have been shattered. Along with all the pots and glasses. To my absolute horror they've destroyed my kettle. Worse, THEY BROKE

MY HIGHLAND COW MUG!

I head upstairs expecting to find just as much mess. My bedroom is destroyed. Someone has set it on fire. Somehow it stayed contained to this room, and has since gone out, but only the charred remains of all my belongings remain. This makes me think magic is at play here.

A roar of anger and annoyance rings from me. I've never made such a noise, but I do believe that the noise is because of my berserker side, that is very much out and making itself known.

Is it possible that whoever has been sending wraiths to try and kill me, have taken this step. Tearing my home apart. But why? What purpose could they possibly have for ruining my home?

"Hi honey, I'm home," I hear Jack call from downstairs.

Of course, that fucker decided to trash my house. Or at least, his presence in my home makes me believe it was him. He was probably thinking if my home was destroyed, I'd be homeless and come crying to him. How wrong he was.

A girly laugh has my blood boiling. Karen. The fucking bitch needs to die. I'd hoped I'd never have to see her fucking botoxified face again. But apparently, I'm not that lucky.

I stroll downstairs as though his being here doesn't bother me. I can't let them know just how much it actually does. On the off chance he didn't hear my roar of rage only a few moments ago, I need him to believe his being alive isn't a problem.

He sees me. The wide grin stretching his face drops at the sight of me and the mace, that I'm glad I wore today. The girls had said I wouldn't need it, since I was just having a girls day, but I'd worn it, wanting to get used to having it on my person. I'm thankful for it now.

"What did you do?" I ask him, ignoring Karen for the time being.

"Ah, just thought I'd ruin you, like you ruined me honey," he says, adding a mask of fake confidence. He's not fooling anyone.

"When did you meet the banshee?" I ask. Giving Karen a passing glance.

"It was actually my lover who made the introductions," He offers, smiling towards Karen.

"Ah, this must be the witch who likes to fuck you in the arse," I remark.

His head whips in my direction. "How do you know that?" he asks, them seems to realise what he said.

"Well, it's an unfortunate accident, that's turned out to have some unexpected benefits. I can talk to sex toys," I giggle. His face seems to go pale when he realises what I'm insinuating.

"Didn't she tell you not to wear it when you met up with the bitch over there," Karen asks Jack. She seems angry and from what I've learnt about banshees over the past week or so, I don't envy Jack right now. Banshees have a scream that has the potential to not only burst your eardrums, but also turn your brain to mush. It's scary but sounds rather interesting.

I'm curious who this mystery woman is. Although Karen mentioned that the person who they're cahooting with told him not to wear a sex toy. How does this person know I can talk to them? It certainly sounds like she's aware of this unique power of mine.

It's someone I'm close to. It has to be. It isn't that common of a knowledge that I can talk to them. Despite us not keeping it secret, I know that most just view it as a joke. They don't actually believe it. Only those I am close with know it's true.

Who told them? How do they know? What witches do I know who have it out for me? None that I can think of, and I've been thinking about it a lot over the past few days.

"Don't fret Karen," a familiar voice says.

Whipping my head around, I find the shy

and unassuming lass, who I thought was my friend. Elana.

I feel more betrayed now, than I did when I found out my family had organised for me to be booted from the town. She'd been so nice and welcoming to me before. Always offering guidance and support. We had girl's nights in, spent laughing and joking. I've always been good at reading people, and I never suspected anything.

"Why?" I ask her. Trying to keep the hurt from my voice.

"You haven't been listening have you," Elana remarks with a sinister grin.

"I've never done anything to hurt you," I say. I have no idea what she's on about when she said I don't listen. She's barely said anything to me, so is it really surprising I don't know what she's on about. Now that I think about it, most of the time she's spoken she's either answering a question I've asked, or she's talking about a past experience but usually about one of the other lasses.

"My parents," she explains.

She'd mentioned today that her parents had been arrested for fighting with a child..., oh. Oh, that's what she means. I was the child.

There were a few incidents with people who weren't students. But I get the feeling it was the couple I fought with.

If I remember right, I'd seen them capturing a rabbit and torturing it. They'd not killed it or hunted it. They had broken its legs. It had been screaming in pain. They'd then proceeded to make cuts on its body. I confronted them and they'd pushed me away.

Me being me, couldn't stand to see an animal in pain, and I knew it was too far gone. So, I'd dived over them and managed to snap the rabbit's neck, killing it instantly. A quick death, rather than a torturous one. I'd hated to have to do it to such an innocent creature, but it was for the best. The couple hadn't been happy and had attacked me. Screaming that I'd messed everything up.

I'd had to fight back because they were full on hitting me and beating me up. I was probably about 13 at the time. Despite it being two against one, I'd managed to hold them off until the police arrived. That was one of the few times I hadn't been arrested. I'd actually been taken to the hospital for a broken arm and ribs.

"My parents are rotting in prison because of you," she screams at me.

Well at least I know what happened to the

couple.

"All I did was defend an innocent creature and then myself. I'm not the one who decided torturing an animal was a good idea. What sort of monsters' torture innocent creatures?" I say, disgusted she would even agree with them. She's sticking up for them by taking it all out on me.

"They weren't bad people," she screams. "The only reason they ended up in that death trap of a prison was because of you. You will pay," she warns.

I look between her, to Karen, and then to Jack. Noticing that Karen is clinging to Jacks arm as though they're close.

"Holy shit," I gasp. All three of them jump at my outburst. "You guys are all sleeping with each other," I state. "I'm surprised that would work. I know Jack can't keep it up for longer than two minutes, and you ladies must be really disappointed," I offer.

It's way off topic, but honestly Elana's threats don't really worry me. I've defeated wraiths before, and I have a feeling I'll be destroying more in the near future. But it's as though my mind has only just put two and two together.

I wonder how that relationship works. Does Elana stick it in Jacks arse, while Jack sticks it up Karen. Do they get Jack off and then get each other off?

"Wait, why do you need Jack? I get you are the witch in charge of raising the wraiths," I say, pointing to Elana, "and you're needed for a power boost," I add, pointing to Karen. "But what do you need Jack for?" I ask.

We had been thinking it was a witch being paid for their service, rather than the witch being the one with the issue. Let's be realistic, she has a fuck ton of issues. But if she's the one with the problem, and Karen obviously hated being smacked down, why is Jack needed?

"You never told her?" Elana asks Jack with a knowing grin.

"Of course not, my love. We aren't supposed to," he offers.

"Jack's a warlock," Elana explains. My eyes go wide. Now that is something that I'd never have guessed.

"So, you just decided to get pay back for the divorce?" I ask him.

"Of course not. My parents are in prison because of you," he remarks.

Another set of parents? That's not right. I've only ever had one couple attack me. There have been adults, but only ever one couple.

"Pretty sure I didn't," I remark.

"My sister and I were extremely displeased about it. So, we decided to play the long game," he offers, smiling towards Elana.

I start gagging.

"Eww, you're taking it up the arse by your own sister?" I ask gobsmacked. "At least now I know why you love Jamie and Cersei Lannister so much."

Urgh. That's just disgusting. I don't have siblings, but Jill is like my sister. I wouldn't ever sleep with her, and I can't imagine what would come over someone, that sleeping with a sibling would be considered a good idea. I gag again, realising I've slept with someone who's been inside his own sister.

"That's just wrong on so many levels," I offer, continuing to gag.

"ENOUGH," Elana screams. "You won't be talking for long. You will pay."

She screams as magic like shadows pours from her. Jack joins in, and a similar magic pours from his body, only his is thicker thanks to Karen's magic. The shadowy mist spreads across the ground in a thick layer and starts to push into the outside.

The ground seems to shake, and a steady

thrum fills the air. The hairs on my body stand up as the air fills with static.

For fucks sake.

When can I just have a normal day?

CHAPTER 30

As the thrum in the air gets louder, my berserker pushes to the surface once again. My muscles seen to bulge as my senses sharpen. She senses the danger and is preparing to fight. I don't even attempt to push her down. With this much power in the room, it's obvious I'm about to fight.

Red magic swirls from Jacks hand, and the front wall of my home disintegrates, letting in the night air. Stood just on the outside are an army of wraiths. At a quick count, there are at least 20 of them. Much to my annoyance, Lucifer lounges on a deck chair, that wasn't there before, along with a stranger. This newcomer looks similar to Lucifer, only he has blonde hair and blue eyes. Just like Lucifer, he has a powerful aura to him. Both sit chilling on lounge chairs, with their feet up, munching on popcorn. They're acting like they're about to watch an exciting show. And I'm the show. Surely, they could, I don't know, help. Fucking pricks.

I'll kill them later.

Ignoring the interlopers, I run through everything I know about wraiths. How to kill them, and all the dangers they possess. My mind flits back to what Sue had said. Kill the witch and you kill the wraiths. Part of me doesn't want to kill either of them. Despite being a violent menace on society, I've never actually killed anyone. I don't want to start now. Obviously, wraiths don't count since they're pretty much zombies. They were dead, and it's only thanks to the jackasses that they're even back.

Turning toward Jack and Elana, I start to run at them. Hopefully knocking them out will accomplish the same thing. Surely if they aren't awake, the magic can't continue.

Apparently, their wraiths are indeed as powerful as mentioned, because they manage to surround me, keeping me from the betrayers.

I pull my maces from their sheathes and prepare to battle. The magic thrumming through my weapons sings to me and fuels my body to fight. They're as bloodthirsty as I am.

Swinging my mace in an arc, I clobber one

in the head. It dents nicely. For the first time in my life, I allow my berserker full freedom, knowing she will be needed. No pulling punches this time. For the first time in my life, I can truly allow my strength to show.

A predatory need fills me and has me bellowing. The call of the fight.

Again, I swing my mace, only this time I shatter a wraiths skull and paint the room red. The spray radius is rather impressive. I swing again, and again I kill a wraith.

Over and over, I swing at the creatures attacking me.

All the while, my mind replays Elana's betrayal. Rose, Jill, and Alexis are her friends, and she didn't just betray me, she betrayed them. Knowing she hurt my friends, my rage increases, until all I think about is destroying the bitch. Another bellow pours from me. My keen senses catch the flinch of the betrayers.

Skull's shatter with each blow. Bones crunch. I sink my teeth into the neck of a wraith who gets too close, and I tear it's throat out, before ripping its head clean off.

One of the maces breaks when my next strike goes through a skull and hits a supporting beam for the house. I didn't think a mace crafted so beautifully would break, but I suppose all weapons have the potential. They certainly weren't created to destroy metal. I throw my other mace to the ground, feeling an urge to destroy with my own bare hands.

I swipe out with my fist, delighting in the crunch of bones, that I can now feel.

Wraith's claw and scratch at me, but it's as though I'm blind to the pain. With each wraith I take down, more seem to replace it. But with each one I take down; I make my way closer and closer to the traitors.

Another bellow escapes me, and my keen senses pick up the arsehole's whimpers. It makes me smile. The predator is hunting its prey.

After what feels like a minute, I finally make my way to Elana. I dive for her. Sinking my teeth into her neck. Blood floods into my mouth, and I unintentionally groan at the taste. It's divine. She screams, and it only fuels my bloodlust. Removing my teeth, I smile at her, allowing some of her blood to pour from my mouth.

"Don't worry, you'll see your parents soon," I promise her, before bashing her gently on the side of the head. It's gentle for me at least. But it's enough force to have her crumpling to the ground in a heap. With the drain of her magic and strength, the wraiths she brought forth also crumple to the ground. Thank god that plan worked.

Jack starts to panic then and tries to escape me. But I tear through the wraiths, blocking the path with ease. Until I can give him the same treatment I gave his lover and sister. I drink until he's weak, before knocking him unconscious.

Since some of the magic is still active, because of Karen, I give her the same treatment. Unfortunately, I take too much blood, and instead of having to bash her on the head, she just crumples to the ground. I'm not even sure if she's still alive. Huh, suppose it doesn't matter either way. Alright I may feel guilty when the adrenaline fades, but for the time being, I couldn't care less.

Since the wraiths are finally down, I look to Lucifer and his companion, who are both finished with their popcorn and cheer loudly at the show they've just witnessed.

I'm surprised to find Xander, my girls, my parents, my grandparents, Hades and Harriot, Dane and a bunch of other guards. They're all watching with the jaws to the ground.

"Hey guys," I offer with a broad smile.

"Uh," Xander offers, unable to get anything else out.

"Well, her transition is complete," Gigi

offers with a beaming smile at me.

I get the feeling I look like a real monster. Blood, and chunks of skull and brain, cake me. Blood stains my chin and neck, and I'm sure I have multiple wounds littering my body. I don't really feel the pain of them though, so I get the feeling the adrenaline is still covering the pain.

"Who are you?" I ask the blonde-haired man beside Lucifer.

"I'm the dickhead upstairs, as you like to call me," he replies.

Ah, God. That makes sense. That also explains why he looks so much like Luci.

Jill comes waltzing up to me without any worry. A grin stretches across her face.

"So, I heard you slept with someone who was having an affair with his sister," she states, cackling like a mad woman.

My head cracks into hers, and she falls to the ground still laughing, but this time rubbing her forehead.

"This is so much better than Game of Thrones," she cackles out. "If they had kids together, would he be both the dad and uncle. Imagine if you'd had kids with him. Their siblings would be the children of incest. That's so fucked up," she adds, wheezing from her laughter.

She isn't even the only one laughing. At least some of them have the decency to try and cover it up. Although, that's mostly the supernatural guards who don't know me well.

CHAPTER 31

After the fight, we all head back to the estate. The betrayers were cuffed with magic dampening cuffs and carted off to a holding cell. I was told there would be trial to decide their sentence but that is it. There guilt has already been witnessed. Due to the nature of the crime, they will likely be sent to the same prison as that of Elana and Jack's parents.

I'm hosed down at the door of the estate, since I'm quite honestly smothered in blood and guts and just about everything else you could imagine. After the hosing, I'm sent to the infirmary to be checked over. Xander forces me to go.

"What have you been up to now?" Healer Rosa asks as soon as she sees me.

I give her a beaming smile. "Oh, you know,

killing wraiths. Beating up betraying arsejackets," I offer.

"Arsejackets?" she questions. "Can't say I've heard that one before."

Before I take a seat on one of the beds, I strip off my clothing, until I'm left in my underwear. Xander is grinning like an idiot, but we both ignore him. His smirk is wiped off his face when the door to the infirmary opens and in walks all my friends and family. They're all chatting excitedly, and I have a feeling it's about what just happened.

Healer Rosa asks if I have any injuries, to which I just shrug. How the hell am I meant to know? Nothing hurts which is typically a sign of not being injured, but I also know that adrenaline is still firing at all angles within me, so there's a good chance I'm just not aware of it.

She does a full check since I have no idea. Surprisingly, I was injured. She mentions that they look like they were pretty deep, but already appear to be healing. This only confirms everyone's suspicions that I've completed my transition. Since my injuries have just about healed, she simply cleans them and lets me go.

"If supernaturals heal this quickly, why do you need an infirmary?" I ask. Surely, they wouldn't have much to do if people heal by themselves in a matter of hours.

"Supernaturals don't heal as quick as you do," Healer Rosa explains.

Is that meant to make sense? I've healed that quick and I'm supernatural.

"Remember what I said," Luci states, and I look to him, confusion screwing up my face. "There are supernaturals, Immortals, and immortal truths," he offers.

Oh. Oh, is he suggesting I'm an immortal.

"What's the difference between immortals and immortal truths?" I ask.

"Both can't be killed easily. We can both survive death, although immortals can be killed with Olympian silver. It's the only way. Immortal truths are different because they have a specific role in life itself. They can only be killed with the soulless sword and even then, it's not quite as simple, there's more steps," he explains. Huh, so they're even hardier than supernaturals.

A past conversation flits through my mind. "Is that what makes mine and Jills family different? Because we're immortals," I ask. I remember someone saying about Jill's and the Heathen family being different to most.

"Yes, sort of," Jill offers. "Our families are made up of immortals and immortal truths," she explains.

"You have immortal truths as well?" I question, unable to figure out who it could possibly be.

"Yea. Mum and dad are," she offers. My jaw drops. "My dad is the Protector and Mum is the Nurturer."

I think about that for a second. That makes a surprising amount of sense. Her dad is the towns sheriff and is very protective of everyone who deserves it. As for her mum, well she's always been caring. Constantly watching out for everyone, but I've noticed she is especially protective of children or those who need it most.

With the all clear given from Healer Rosa, I hop up from the bed. Jill and I walk together, with the rest of our friends and family strolling along behind us. Why they insist on staying close by, is beyond me, but I allow it for now. It almost seems like they're waiting for something, but I've no idea what.

"So, you mated with Xander," Jills states rather than questions.

"I did," I offer.

"I'm surprised. I expected you to fight it more," she reveals.

"I was going to. But then I realised I never

felt like this with Jack. I've been attached to Xander more than I have any other person. I also figured that if he pisses me off, I'll just kill him," I smile brightly. She snorts at that.

We head up to Xanders room. Since there are too many of us to fit in the lift, some wait for the next one. Once everyone is upstairs, we make our way to Xander's room. I start to get suspicious. Why is everyone following us?

"What's going on?" I ask the crowd.

"Nothing. Go get a shower, ready for your fitting," Xander orders.

I frown.

"What fitting?" I ask.

"Dress fitting," he states.

I frown.

"What dress fitting?" I ask.

"The one you're booked in for. You need a dress for your coronation, or are you planning on going in your underwear," Xander asks.

My mind promptly fizzles out. I'm having a coronation? Since when? I know I'm Xanders mate, but I didn't think that would automatically make me queen, and I certainly didn't think it would require a coronation.

When my family and friends seem to

lean forward with their eyes shining with expectation, I realise why they had followed. They wanted to see my reaction. They're expecting fireworks.

Should I be reacting poorly to this. A coronation is a big thing, but at the same time, it can't be as bad as orgasming in a room full of supernaturals, from a ceremony that was meant to be painful. Then again, I'm not entirely sure what that ceremony was meant to do, since I've yet to feel very connected to anyone from the estate.

"Okay," I offer calmly. When frowns mar the faces of my friends and family, I get all the confirmation I need. They were expecting me to freak out. But I didn't. "Also, what was that ceremony meant to do? The one that was meant to be painful," I ask Xander.

"It was meant to connect you with those of the estate. It didn't work however, and we aren't entirely sure why. You should be able to communicate telepathically, but we've tried, and nothing gets through to you," he explains.

Huh, I wonder why it didn't work. Xander shrugs his shoulders, telling me he has no idea why it didn't work either.

Instead of dwelling on all the shit that's not important, I take myself to the bathroom and take a quick shower. At least it was meant to be quick. Apparently, blood and guts... and... well, everything else, is pretty difficult to remove. It takes a while for me to clean everything off, but eventually manage and hurry to get dried.

Having forgotten to grab any clothing before my shower, I wrap my towel securely around me. I'm not sure if everyone has left, or if they're still chilling with Xander, but I don't worry about it. I'm either related to them, friends with them, or they've already seen me naked, so I don't see it as a big deal. Even more so since, I am in a towel, it's not like anything is actually on show.

Once I've got some underwear on, I wrap a bathrobe around me. I don't want to get changed if I'm only going to strip them off again in a few minutes.

True to my beliefs the family had decided to stay in Xanders accommodations. All of them spread throughout the living area as though they haven't a care in the world. They laugh and joke, offering jabs at one another.

How did I go from having no family there for me, to having a huge family who care so much about me?

Xander leaves our family in favour of showing me to the fitting room on the 2nd floor of the estate. We're greeted at the door of the closed shop. It would seem we have an appointment. Xander leaves me in the capable hands of the employees, and they lead me into the centre of the room. Rooms spread around the store, but in the centre is a large podium. My guess is this is usually used as a podium for someone to show the dress off to their friends and families. Today however, it's not being used for that purpose.

Since the blinds on the shop are drawn, I'm asked to put on a gown and stand on the podium. It seems I don't even have a say in the gown I'm to wear, but I actually don't mind. Since I've never been a big fan of dresses, not liking the restrictive aspect of the ones Jack liked, the employees likely have more idea on what would suit me.

The four employees, three women and a man, scuttle about pinning and tucking the dress into place. They add and remove fabric to their hearts content.

The dress is unzipped, and I step out of it awkwardly. Trying to avoid getting pricked by the hundreds of pins that have been added to the gown. My bathrobe is handed to me, and I'm led to a comfortable chair. I'm told to wait there for the men to come and doll me up.

About five minutes later, there's a knock at the door. An employee from the dress shop opens it up, and two handsome men come strolling in. One is a large muscular man, while the other is Mal, a supernatural who helped me that day in the cemetery.

They both come over to me and make quick work of setting up their equipment. As soon as they're ready, Mal gets to work trimming my hair, while his friend starts cutting and buffing my nails.

"Are you excited about tomorrow?" Mal asks.

"What's going on tomorrow?" I ask. An uncomfortable feeling settles in my gut. Why do I worry I know what he's going to say.

The man sorting my nails out, smirks up at me. "The coronation," he confirms.

Urgh! For fucks sake. "Just how long has this damn thing been planned for?" I ask.

"About a week. Similar time to when it was thought you would die," Mal offers with a chuckle. "Well, die for the third time. Honestly you need to quit doing that," he offers, and I snort.

"Right, of course it's been planned for a while. Not like I needed to be told about it sooner," I mutter.

"They didn't want to give you the time to freak out about it. You're not exactly the most level-headed of people," the man offers.

"Chris, honey, don't start winding her up," Mal warns with amusement in his voice.

"Wait, you two are partners?" I ask, surprised. "I thought Hades was the gay one in your group," I explain.

"He is too," Mal offers with a chuckle.

"Oh, I'm aware," I say seriously. Chris, the man doing my nails frowns at me in question. "Ask him about Abaddon the destroyer," I order with a beaming smile.

It takes the men about 60 minutes to finish their work. By the end, my nails are decorated and painted in blacks and whites. A beautiful, webbed design is painted on, and I stare transfixed at the beauty.

My hair was trimmed and curled in preparation for tomorrow. Mal did say I needn't worry about sleeping on it, since it will mostly be up, but the curls will help with the volume, not that I need much help on that account. But it also allowed him to test my hair's ability with curls, since not everyone's curls well, just like not everyone straightens well.

Once that's done, I'm pushed back into the dress that has been stitched, and fabrics added, while others have been removed. They make some final alterations and add pins or accessories.

Finally, I'm allowed to leave. If dress fittings are usually that long and tiresome, then I hope there is never another occasion for that to be needed again.

I collapse into bed that night, and for the first time in a while, I feel whole and happy. With a man who loves me wrapping me securely in his arms, and a family I know love me beyond all measure, as well as friends I can turn to, I drift off into a peaceful and content sleep.

I need my rest after all. I've got my coronation tomorrow.

CHAPTER 32

The following day is hectic. Xander leaves early in the morning to make preparations for the coronation. I'm ordered to get washed, and await the stylists, as well as my dress, to arrive. I'd be lying if I said I wasn't disappointed about not getting some alone time with Xander before today. Now that we've done it once, I'm addicted and want him every hour of the day. But beggars can't be choosers and it would seem he's too busy for me.

A hearty breakfast is brought to my room. The tray has a stack of pancakes with bacon and sausage on it, as well as a jug of syrup. A pot of tea is also on the tray, which I'm thankful for, as I live off the stuff. What surprises me the most is the glass of crimson fluid. Blood. It's still taking some getting used to my new diet. I love blood but my human conditioning always makes me see the consumption of blood as wrong.

I've also found that I prefer Xanders blood above all else. But again, beggars can't be choosers. I hope he realises that he's going to be in for it later, when we finally get some time for one another.

Just as I'm finishing up my meal, a knock rings on the door. Opening it, I find the employees of the dress shop, as well as Mal and Chris. Even more surprising is Hades, Jill, Alexis and Rosemary. They all carry a dress bag and squeal in excitement, including Hades.

The morning is filled with excited chatter, while our hair is styled, and makeup is applied. Everyone works together, helping one another out, but most focus on making sure I'm ready.

By the time of the coronation at 8pm, I'm dolled up and almost unrecognisable. But not in a bad way. They've managed to dress me and make me up to accentuate my natural beauty and not make me into something else.

The dress makers, as well as Mal and Chris, leave before the coronation to get ready by themselves.

Hades, Jill, Alexis and Rosemary stay with me. We walk steadily down to the ground floor where the large ballroom is. I've not been in there since the welcoming ball.

When we make it to the large, imposing, Mahogany doors, we are stopped by the guards who inform me to wait until everyone is situated. The wait has bats flapping in my gut, as my nerves pick up. It isn't helped when memories of the ceremony from hell, surface. Please don't let me orgasm in front of everyone again.

It seems like an eternity until the guards are informed to open the doors.

My friends make sure my long black and purple dress is placed properly before stepping to the sides.

I'm actually surprised how much I love the dress. It's a form fitting bodice, that's actually a corset, done in black material, with purple lace delicately applied on top. The skirt of the dress is heavy and large, but it's not over the top. Again, it's black but has the purple lace details that add a dainty side to it. On top on the dress is a cape that is just as delicate and has a train that runs a fair bit. In my opinion it's too long but even I can admit that it does work with the overall look, which is the only reason I didn't complain too much.

My hair has been braided in parts and left down in others. Viking braids is what Mal and Chris called them. I love the entire look, and I'm impressed with the talent of those who made something so perfect for me.

The doors to the grand ballroom are pulled open. A carpeted runway has been set up running through the room, leaving people of either side of it. It's purple. It's the same purple as the lace detailing on my dress.

Holding my head high, I start walking down the aisle. My eyes spot Xander at the front. A look of pure adoration fills his features, and it's him that I focus on. I really don't like everyone watching me intently, but looking at Xander, the world slips away, until it's just him and me in the room. It doesn't take too long to reach the front, although I follow the instructions given to me by my friends. They told me to take my time when walking. I don't want to be too long, but I also don't want to be too quick. We'd practiced.

Once at the front, I look up to my husband on the slight podium. He's dressed in a well-made three-piece suit. Just like my dress and the carpet, purple decorates it with intricate stitched in details, that was likely done by hand. The crown that sits on his head glitters in the light, and manages to match Xander, rather than looking like an odd piece added.

I've been warned a supernatural coronation is slightly different to what humans do. It's almost like a marriage to the community. You're seen more as being there to support the people, rather than being an absent leader.

"Welcome to all," Xander starts, addressing the room. He then proceeds to talk about the history of the supernatural royals and emphasises the importance of such a role. He talks about how they've been in power for years, after being voted in, centuries ago. Just like those royals of the past, the current rulers strive to be fair and just, in everything they do. He talks about how peace had been gained through the rulers of the supernatural.

Finally, he gets to the main part. "Do you Freyja Eliza Heathen promise to be fair and responsible in ruling the supernatural race?"

"I do," I confirm.

"Do you promise to listen to your people to enact justice and support where needed?"

"I do," I confirm.

"Do you promise to work to maintain a peaceful and prosperous community?"

"I do," I confirm.

"Does anyone have any reasons why Freyja Eliza Heathen should not be crowned?" Xander asks the room.

The room remains silent, much to my

surprise.

"I crown thee, Freyja Eliza Heathen," Xander states, as I kneel down. He places a crown on my head. "Rise, Queen Freyja Eliza Heathen," he orders, and I stand.

Xander helps me up the steps of the podium and I turn to face everyone.

"Praise be the Queen," Xander states.

"Praise be the Queen," everyone in the room responds.

A cheer rises in the room as Xander and I stand at the front. A shy smile stretches my face as I realise that people do in fact like me. Despite my oddities and anger issues, they like me. They seem happy and excited that I'm queen. It's surprising.

The room settles down when Xanders father and mother step forward.

"Rumours have been spreading about our new Queen," his mother states. I'd met her a couple days ago, only briefly. Her name is Florence, or Flo as she prefers. "We would like to dispel those rumours," she explains.

I haven't heard any rumours, so this is all news to me. But something tells me it's something big. It's as though everyone holds their breaths in anticipation.

We turn towards the large mahogany doors at the entrance of the ballroom, where Jill walks down the aisle, holding a dagger cautiously in her hands.

Behind her, the immortal truths follow. My mother, father, Gigi, Papi, Mark and Eve, God, as well as a couple of people I haven't met. They reach the front of the room where Jill walks up onto the podium, while the immortal truths remain on ground level.

"This is the Dagger of the Truths," Jill explains, holding up the simple, but deadly dagger. Even from here I can see the sharpness of the blade. Despite its simplicity, I can also spot some intricate designs etched into the blade of the weapon. I'm hoping I get a closer look at the weapon, I bet it is something to truly behold. "It is a test. When it comes into contact with the blood of an immortal truth, a symbol will light up, speaking of the truth that immortal represents," she explains. I'm wondering why she has it.

Jill turns to me and Xander steps away from me.

"Do you consent to the test of the immortal truths?" she asks.

I've no idea why I should say no, so I don't. "I consent," I say.

Is this what everyone was wondering

about? Do they honestly think I'm an immortal truth? Surely that can't be the case. Just a few months ago I had no idea that the supernatural were real. Now I've only just completed my transition and I'm still learning what everything in the community is. Surely, they are out of their minds thinking I'm a truth. I'm just waiting for them to realise, and this test will prove it.

Jill nods her head and asks for my hand. I place it palm up in her hand. She places the blade on my palm and slices across. I don't even flinch. It's the least painful thing I've had happen to me, ever. So it's not like I'm going to complain.

My blood pools on my palm, and Jill presses the blade gently into the blood.

Almost instantly a symbol lights up. It's a symbol of a sword smothered in flame.

"Welcome the immortal truth, Wrath," Jill shouts, and another cheer rings through the air. My family look up at me with huge grins on their faces, and it takes more than a moment for it to truly sink in.

I'm an immortal truth. Just like my parents and grandparents. I'm the queen of the supernatural. I have the love of my life by my side. Now, I'm the immortal truth representative of wrath.

That's certainly fitting for me, but it still

going to take some getting used to.

After the ceremonies, music fills the room, and the celebration truly begins. Xander holds his hand out to me and leads me to the dance floor. I've no idea how to dance, but he leads the way with a skill I've never seen. Who knew the man could dance?

"You look stunning," he states, and he holds me close.

"You look as handsome as always, although the regal attire certainly gives me ideas," I offer. You should know by now my love language is sarcasm. If not sarcasm, then a compliment with some extras.

Xander laughs and gives me a kiss that steals my breath.

After our dance, my father takes my hand, and he too leads me in a dance. He offers compliments and delights in being allowed to hug me.

My family take turns dancing with me, until eventually, Lucifer comes waltzing over. He takes my hand and spins me around in a rather energetic dance, that has me tripping over my own feet.

"You look lovely, my devilish little niece," he offers. The sly smile stretching his face, warns me of incoming trouble. "I'm surprised you can actually look dignified. I'm guessing magic was needed, maybe an attitude adjustment as well," he goads.

True to form, I beat the living snot out of him. He laughs the entire time, as do I. It isn't until we've finished brawling that I realise I needed it. I needed the release of my pent-up nerves. Even more impressive is that I didn't ever damage my dress, although the crown fell off rather quickly and was picked up by Xander, who has a broad grin on his face.

As Lucifer leaves me, he gives me a slight nod of his head. He knew. He knew I needed a release, and well, no one would care about me beating up the Devil. He really is a masochist, because he wasn't one bit bothered about the beating.

Jill comes bounding over, stating, "Well I'm glad you beat him up. That man pisses me off." I raise my brow at her. Since when does Jill let anyone get under her skin. She somewhat level-headed, especially compared to me.

"What's he done to bother you?" I ask.

"He's the devil, does he even need a reason," she remarks.

The man we speak of, turns to look at us and blows us a kiss. At first, I think it's aimed at both Jill and me, but then I focus closer. He's looking at Jill.

The devil just blew Jill a kiss.

Well, that's a story I need to know!

AFTERWORD

If you enjoyed this story follow me on Facebook to keep up to date on upcoming releases.

Facebook: Mollie Sykes Author

Email: MollieSykesAuthor@hotmail.com

Printed in Great Britain
by Amazon

40769740R00192